G. J. Wl

MW01673860

The Gladiators

A Tale of Rome and Judaea. In three volumes. Vol. 2

SALZWASSER VERLAG

G. J. Whyte Melville

The Gladiators

A Tale of Rome and Judaea. In three volumes. Vol. 2

Reprint of the original, first published in 1863.

1st Edition 2022 | ISBN: 978-3-37500-378-4

Verlag (Publisher): Salzwasser Verlag GmbH, Zeilweg 44, 60439 Frankfurt, Deutschland
Vertretungsberechtigt (Authorized to represent): E. Roepke, Zeilweg 44, 60439 Frankfurt, Deutschland
Druck (Print): Books on Demand GmbH, In de Tarpen 42, 22848 Norderstedt, Deutschland

THE GLADIATORS:

A Tale of Rome and Judæa.

BY

G. J. WHYTE MELVILLE

IN THREE VOLUMES.

VOL. II.

LONDON

1863.

CONTENTS.

VOL. II.

ANTEROS.

THE GLADIATORS.

VOL. II.

ANTEROS.

CHAPTER I.

THE LISTENING SLAVE.

WOUNDED, vanquished, transferred from his kind master, and further from liberty than ever, Esca's was now indeed a pitiable lot. The Tribune, entitled, by the very terms of his wager, to the life and person of his antagonist, was not the man to forego this advantage by any act of uncalled-for generosity. In the Briton, he believed he now possessed a tool to use with effect, in furtherance of a work, which the seductive image of Valeria rendered every day more engrossing: an auxiliary by whose aid he might eventually stand first in the good graces of the only woman who had ever obtained a mastery over his unyielding disposition and selfish heart. None the more on this account did he cherish the captive, nor alleviate his condition as a slave. From the effects of his injury, Esca could not be put to any harder kinds of labour, but in all menial offices, however degrading, he was compelled to take his share. Different, indeed, was his condition here from what it had been in the service of the high-minded Licinius, and bitterly did he feel the exchange.

Submitting to sarcasm, insult, continued ill-treatment and annoyance, the noble barbarian would have failed under the trial, had it not been for a few well-remembered words, on the truth of which Calchas had so often insisted, and in which —(for when were human thoughts without an earthly leavening?) Mariamne seemed to cherish an implicit belief. Those words breathed hope and consolation under the very worst misfortunes that life could offer; and Esca suffered on, very silent, and tolerably patient, although, perhaps, there was a fiercer fire smouldering in his breast than would have been approved by his venerable monitor,—a fire that only waited occasion to blaze out all the more dangerously for being thus forcibly suppressed.

With a malicious pleasure, natural to his disposition, Placidus compelled the Briton to perform several domestic offices which brought him about his person. It flattered the Tribune's vanity to have continually before his eyes the athletic frame he was so proud to have overcome, and it pleased him that his friends, guests, and clients should be thus led to converse upon his late encounter, which had created no small gossip in the fashionable world of Rome. It happened then, that Esca, while preparing his master's bath, was startled to hear the name that was never long out of his own thoughts spoken in accents of secresy and caution by the Tribune himself, who was in the adjoining apartment, holding close consultation with Hippias the fencing-master, and the two freedmen, Damasippus and Oarses. All were obviously interested in the subject under discussion, and, believing themselves safe from eavesdroppers, spoke energetically, though in tones somewhat lower than their wont.

He started, and the blood ebbed painfully from his heart. "Mariamne!" yes, the word was again repeated, and while Oarses said something in a whisper, he could clearly distinguish the Tribune's low, mocking laugh.

It was plain they were unaware of his presence, and, indeed, it was at an earlier hour than usual that he had made ready the unguents, perfumes, strigil, and other appliances indispensable to the luxurious ablutions of a Roman patrician. The bath-room was inside the favourite apartment of Placidus, where he was now holding counsel, and could only be entered through the latter, from which it was separated by a heavy velvet curtain. Esca, surrounded by the materials of the toilet, had been sitting for a longer time than he knew, lost in thought, until aroused by the mention of Mariamne's name. Thus it was that the four others believed the bath-room empty, and their conversation unheard.

Anxious and excited, the Briton scarcely dared to draw his breath, but crept cautiously behind the folds of the heavy curtain, and listened attentively.

The Tribune was walking to and fro with the restless motions and stealthy gait of a tiger in its cage. Hippias, seated at his ease upon a couch, was examining the device of a breastplate, with his usual air of good-humoured superiority, and Damasippus, appealing with admiring looks to Oarses, who responded in kind, seemed to endorse, as it were, with a dependent's mute approval, the opinions and observations of his patron.

"Two-thirds of the Legions have already come over," said Placidus, rapidly enumerating the forces on which Vespasian's party could count. "In Spain, in Gaul, in Britain, the soldiers have declared openly against Vitellius. The surrender of Cremona can no longer be concealed from the meanest populace. Alexandria, the granary of the empire, has fallen into the hands of Vespasian. Those dusky knaves, thy countrymen, Oarses, will see us starve, ere they send us supplies under the present dynasty; and think ye our greasy plebeians here will endure the girdle of famine, thus drawn tighter, day by day, round their luxurious paunches? The fleet at Misenum was secured long ago, but the news that Cæsar could not count upon a single galley in blue water, only reached the capital to-day. Then the old Prætorians are ripe for mischief: you may trust them never to forget nor to forgive the disgrace of last year, when the chosen band was broke, dismissed, and, worst of all, deprived of rations and pay

I tell thee, Hippias, those angry veterans are ready to take the town without assistance, and put old and young to the sword. Fail! it is impossible we can fail, the new party outnumbers the old by ten to one!"

"You have told off a formidable list," replied Hippias, quietly; "I cannot see that you are in need of any further help from me or mine."

Placidus shot a sharp, questioning glance at the fencing-master, and resumed.

"Half the numbers that have given in their adhesion to Vespasian would serve to put my chariot-boy on the throne. Automedon's long curls might be bound by a diadem to-morrow, were he the favourite of the hour, so far as Rome is concerned. You know what the masses are, my Hippias, for it is your trade to pander to their tastes, and rouse their enthusiasm. It is true that the great general is, at this moment, virtually ruler of the empire, but a pebble might turn the tide in the capital. I would not trust Vespasian's own son, young and dissipated as he is, could he but make a snatch at the reins with any hope of holding them firmly, when once within his grasp. Titus Flavius Domitian might be emperor to-morrow, if he would be satisfied to wear the purple but for a week, and then make room for some one else. Nay, the people are fickle enough to be capable of turning round at any moment, and retaining our present admirable ruler on the throne. Rome must be coerced, my Hippias; the barbers, and cobblers, and water-carriers must be kept down and intimidated; if need be, we must cut a few garlick-breathing throats. It may be necessary to remove Cæsar himself, lest the reactionary feeling should burst out again, and we should find ourselves left with nothing for our pains, but the choice of a cup of poison, a gasp in a halter, or three inches of steel. We *must* succeed this time, for not a man need hope for pardon if Cæsar is thoroughly frightened. Hippias, there must be no half-measures now!"

"Well said!" exclaimed the freedmen in a breath, with very pale faces, nevertheless, and an enthusiasm obviously somewhat against the grain.

Hippias looked quietly up from the breast-plate resting on his lap.

"There will be shows," said he, "and blood flowing like water in the Circus, whoever wears the purple. While Rome stands, the gladiator need never want for bread."

"Now you speak like a man of sense," replied

the Tribune, in the same tone. "For after all, the whole matter resolves itself into a mere question of money. The shows are tolerably lucrative, at least to their contriver, but it takes many a festival ere the sesterces count by tens of thousands; and Hippias loves luxury and wine, and women, too, —nay, deny it not, my comely hero; and if the Family and their trainer could be hired at a fair price, for an hour's work or so, why they need never enter the arena again, save as spectators; nay, poorer men than their chief might be, have sat in the equestrian rows, ere now."

"You want to hire my chickens and myself for a forlorn hope," retorted Hippias, impatiently. "Better say so at once, and be plain with me."

"It is even so," resumed Placidus, with an assumption of extreme candour. "For real work I have few I can depend upon but the old Prætorians; and though they stick at nothing, there are hardly enough of them for my purpose. With a chosen two hundred of thine, my dealer in heroes, I could command Rome for twenty-four hours; and when Placidus soars into the sky, he carries Hippias on his wings. Speak out; thy terms are high, but such a game as ours is not played for a handful of pebbles, or a few brass farthings. What is the price, man by man?"

"You would require two hundred of them," observed the other, reflectively. "Five thousand sesterces* a man, and his freedom, which would come to nearly as much more."

"The killed not to count, of course," bargained the Tribune.

"Of course not," repeated Hippias. "Listen, most illustrious; I will take all chances, and supply the best men I have, for eight thousand a head. Two hundred swordsmen who would take Pluto by the beard without a scruple, if I only lifted my hand. Lads who can hold their own against thrice their number of any legion that was ever drilled. They are ready at two hours' notice."

He was speaking truth, for Hippias was honest enough in his own particular line. Amongst the thousands who owed their professional standing, and the very bread they ate, to the celebrated fencing-master, it was no hard task to select a company of dare-devils, such as he described, who would desire no better sport than to see their native city in flames, with the streets knee-deep in

* About forty pounds sterling.

blood and wine, while they put men, women, and children, indiscriminately to the sword. The Tribune's eye brightened, as he thought of the fierce work he could accomplish with such tools as these ready to his hand.

"Keep them for me, from to-day," he answered, looking round the apartment, as though to assure himself that he was only heard by those in his confidence. "My plan cannot but succeed if we only observe common secresy and caution. Ten picked men, and thyself, my Hippias, I bid to sup with me here, the rest of the band shall be distributed by twenties amongst the different streets opening on the Palace, preserving their communication thus,—one man at a time must continually pass from each post to the next, until every twenty has been changed. This secures us from treachery, and will keep our cut-throats on the alert. At a given signal, all are to converge on the middle garden-gate, which will be found open. Then they may lead the old Prætorians to the attack, and take the palace itself by assault, in defiance of any resistance, however desperate, that can be made. The German guard are stubborn dogs, and must be put to the sword directly the outer hall is gained. I would not have them burn down the palace if they can help it; but when they have done *my* work, they are welcome to all they can carry out of it on their backs, and you may tell them so."

Hippias noted in his own mind this additional incentive with considerable satisfaction. After a moment's pause, he looked fixedly in the Tribune's face, and inquired,

"How would you wish your guests armed for the supper-party? Shall we bring our knives with us, kind host?"

Placidus flushed a dark red, and then grew pale. He averted his eyes from Hippias, while he answered,

"There are few weapons so true as the short, two-edged sword. There will be work for our brave little party inside the Palace, of which we must make no bungling. Is it such a grave matter, my Hippias, to slay a fat old man?" he added, inquiringly.

The other's face assumed an expression of intense disgust.

"Nay," said he, "I will have no murder done in cold blood. As much fighting as you please, in the way of business, but we are no hired assassins, my men and I. To put one Cæsar off the throne, and another on, is a pretty night's amusement enough, and I have no objection to it; but to take an old man out of his bed, even though he be an emperor, and slay him as you slay a fat sheep, I'll none of it. Send for a butcher, Tribune, this is no trade of ours!"

Placidus bit his lip, and seemed to think profoundly for a moment, then his brow cleared, and he resumed with a light laugh.

"Far be it from me to offend a gladiator's scruples. I know the morals of the Family, and respect their prejudices. Half the money shall be in your hands within an hour: the rest shall be paid when the job is done. I think we understand each other well enough. Is it a bargain, Hippias? Can I depend upon you?"

The fencing-master was not yet satisfied. "About the guests?" he asked, sternly. "How are we to pay for our supper?"

Placidus clapped him on the shoulder, with a jovial laugh. "I will be frank with thee," said he, "old comrade. Why should there be secrets between thee and me? We go from my supper-table to the Palace. We enter with the storming-party. I know the private apartments of the Emperor. I can lead our little band direct to the royal presence. Here we will rally round Vitellius, and take his sacred person into our charge. Hippias, I will make it ten thousand sesterces a man, for each of the ten, and thou shalt name thine own price for thine own services. But the Emperor must not escape. Dost thou understand me now?"

"I like it not," replied the other; "but the price is fair enough, and my men must live. I would it could be so arranged that some resistance might be made in the palace: you slay a man so much easier with his helmet on and his sword in his hand!"

"Pooh! prejudice!" laughed the Tribune. "Professional fancies that spring from thy coarse, material trade. Blood leaves no more stain than wine. You and I have spilt enough of both in our time. What matter, a throat cut, or a cracked flagon of Falernian? Dash a pitcher of water over a marble floor like this, and you wash away the signs of both at once. Said I not well, Damasippus? Why, what ails thee, man? Thy face has turned as white as thy gown!"

Damasippus, indeed, whose eyes were fixed upon the floor to which his patron had just alluded. presented, at this juncture, an appearance of intense terror and amazement. The freedman's mouth was open, his cheeks were deadly pale, and his very hair seemed to bristle with dismay. Pointing a shaking finger to the slabs of marble at his feet, he could only stammer out in broken accents, "May the gods avert the omen!" over and over again.

The others, following the direction of his gaze, were no less astonished to see a narrow stream of crimson winding over the smooth, white floor, as though the very stones protested against the Tribune's reckless and inhuman sentiments. For an instant all stood motionless, then Placidus, leaping at the velvet curtain, tore it fiercely open, and discovered the cause of the phenomenon.

Listening attentively for some further mention of the name that had roused his whole being, not a syllable of the foregoing conversation had been lost upon Esca, who, kneeling on one knee, with his wounded foot bent under him, and his ear applied close to the heavy folds of the curtain, had never moved a hair's-breadth from his attitude of fixed and absorbing attention.

In this constrained position, the wound in his foot, which was not yet healed over, had opened afresh, and though he was himself unconscious of all but the cruel and treacherous scheme he overheard, it bled so freely, that a dark stream stole gradually beneath the curtains, and crept gently along the marble to the very feet of the horror-stricken Damasippus.

Esca sprang to his full height. In that moment his blood curdled, as it had done when he was down upon the sand, with his enemy's eye glaring on him through the cruel net. He knew the Tribune, and he felt there was no hope.

The latter laughed loud and long. It was his way of covering all disagreeable emotions, but it boded no good to the object of his mirth.

When Esca heard that laugh he looked anxiously about him as though to seek a weapon. What was the use? He stood wounded and defenceless in the power of four reckless men, of whom two were armed.

"Hold him!" exclaimed Placidus to his freedmen, drawing at the same time a short two-edged sword from its sheath. "It is unfortunate for the barbarian that he has learned our language. The necessity is disagreeable, but there is only one way of insuring silence. My bath too is prepared so I can spare him for to-day, and my freedmen will see that his place is supplied by to-morrow.

Hold him, cowards! I say; do you fear that he will bite you?"

Neither Damasippus nor Oarses, however, seemed much inclined to grapple with the stalwart Briton. Wounded and outnumbered as he was, without a chance of rescue or escape, there was yet a defiant carriage of the head, a fierce glare in the eye, that warned the freedmen to keep hands off him as long as they could. They looked at each other irresolutely, and shrank from the patron's glance.

That moment's hesitation saved him. Hippias, who regarded every six feet of manhood with a brave heart inside it as his own peculiar property, had besides a kindly feeling for his old pupil. He put his muscular frame between the master and the slave.

"Give him a day or two, Tribune," said he, carelessly. "I can find a better use for him than to cut his throat here on this clean white floor, and an equally safe one in the end, you may be sure."

"Impossible, fool!" answered Placidus, angrily. "He has heard enough to destroy every hair on the head of each of us. He must never leave this room alive!"

"Only twenty-four hours," pleaded the fencing-master, who well knew how much at that time in Rome a day might bring forth. "Put him in ward as close as you will, but let him live till to-morrow. Hippias asks it as a favour to himself, and you may not like to be refused by him, when it is *your* turn. What if I should say No—in the private apartments of the palace? Come, let us make a compromise."

The Tribune reflected for a moment. Then striking his right hand into that of Hippias, "Agreed!" said he. "Twenty-four hours' grace on one side, and the sharpest blade in Rome at my disposal on the other. Ho! Damasippus, call some of my people in. Bid them put the new collar on the slave, and chain him to the middle pillar in the inner court."

The order was punctually obeyed, and Esca found himself a helpless prisoner burdened with a secret that might save the empire, and with maddening apprehensions on behalf of Mariamne tearing at his heart.

CHAPTER II.

"ATTACK AND DEFENCE."

SUCH beauty as the Jewess's, although she seldom went abroad, and led as sequestered a life as was compatible with the domestic duties she had to perform, could not pass unnoticed in a place like Rome.

Notwithstanding the utter contempt in which her nation was held by its proud conquerors, she had been observed going to market in the morning for the few necessaries of her household, or filling her pitcher from the Tiber at sunset; and amongst other evil eyes that had rested on her fair young face were those of Damasippus, freedman to Julius Placidus the Tribune. He had lost no time in reporting to his patron the jewel he had discovered, so to speak, in its humble setting;

for, like the jackal, Damasippus never dared to hunt for himself, and followed after evil, not for its own sake, but for the lust of gold.

His patron too, though he had only seen the girl once, and then closely veiled, was so inflamed by the description of her charms, on which the client dwelt at great length, that he resolved to possess himself of her, in the sheer insolence of a great man's whim, promising the freedman, that after the lion was served he should have the jackal's reward. It was in consequence of this agreement that a plot was laid of which Esca overheard but half a dozen syllables, and yet enough to render him very uneasy when he reflected on the recklessness and cruelty of him with whom it originated, and the slavish obedience with which it was sure to be carried out. It would have broken the spirit of a brave man to be chained to a pillar, fasting and wounded, with only twenty-four hours to live; and a keen suspicion that the woman he loved was even then all unconsciously walking into the toils, added a pang to bodily suffering which might have turned the stoutest heart to water, but Esca never lost hope altogether. Something he could not analyze seemed to give him comfort and support, nor was he aware that the blind vague trust he was beginning to entertain in some power above, and beyond himself, yet on which he felt he could implicitly rely, was the first glimmer of the true faith dawning on his soul.

Perhaps the slave in his chain, under sentence of death, bore a lighter heart than his luxurious master, washed, perfumed, and tricked out in all the glitter of dress and ornament, rolling in his gilded chariot to do homage to the woman who had really mastered his selfish heart.

Automedon, whose eyes were of the sharpest, remarked that his lord was nervous and restless, that his cheek paled, and his lip shook more and more as they proceeded on their well-known way, and that when they neared the portals of Valeria's house the Tribune's hand trembled so that he could scarcely fasten the brooch upon his shoulder. How white against the crimson mantle, dyed twice and thrice, till it had deepened almost into purple, looked those uncertain fingers, quivering about the clasp of gold!

However reckless, unprincipled, and cunning a man may be, he is inevitably disarmed by the woman he really loves. This is even the case when his affection is returned; but when he has fallen into the hands of one who, disliking him personally, has resolved to make him her tool, his situation is pitiable indeed. These hopeless passions, too, have in all ages been of the fiercest, and the most enduring. Ill usage on the one side or the other has not produced the effect that might be expected, and the figurative shirt of Nessus, instead of being torn off in shreds and cast away, has been far oftener hugged closer and closer to the skin, burning and blistering into the very marrow.

It generally happens, too, that the suitor, whose whole existence seems to hang upon his success, blunders into the course that leads him in a direction exactly contrary to his goal. He is pretty sure to say and do the wrong thing at the wrong time. He offers his attentions with a pertinacity that wearies and offends, or withdraws them with a precipitation so transparent as to compel remark. When he should be firm he is plaintive, when he is expected to be cheerful, he turns sulky. To enhance his own value, he becomes boastful to the extreme verge, and sometimes beyond it, of the truth; or in order to prove his devotion, he makes himself ridiculous, and thereby deals the final and suicidal blow, if such indeed be necessary, that is to shatter like glass the fabric of his hopes.

The Tribune knew women thoroughly. He could plead no lack of experience, for ignorance of that intricate and puzzling labyrinth, a woman's heart. He had indeed broken more than one in the process of examination, and yet the boy Automedon, sitting by his side in the chariot, with the wind lifting his golden curls, would hardly have been guilty of so many false movements, such mistakes both of tactics and strategy, as disgraced his lord's conduct of the unequal warfare he waged with Valeria. Yet this engrossing affection, stained and selfish as it was, constituted perhaps the one redeeming quality of the Tribune's character, afforded the only incentive by which his better and manlier feelings could be aroused.

Possibly Valeria expected him. Women have strange instincts on such matters, which seldom deceive. She was dressed with the utmost magnificence, as though conscious that simplicity could have no charms for Placidus, and sat in a splendour nearly regal, keeping Myrrhina and the rest of her maidens within call. Lovers are acute observers; as he walked up the cool spacious court to greet her, he saw that she was gentler, and more languid than her wont; she looked wearied and unhappy, as though she, too, acknowledged the sorrows and the weaknesses of her sex. Lover-like, he thought this unusual shade of softness became her well.

For days she had been fighting with her own heart, and she had suffered as such undisciplined natures must. The strife had left its traces on her pale proud face, and she felt a vague unacknowledged yearning for repose. The wild bird had beat her wings and ruffled her plumage till she was tired, and a skilful fowler would have taken advantage of the reaction to lure her into his net.

Perhaps she had been thinking what happiness it must be to have one in the world in whom she could confide, on whom she could rely; one loyal manly nature on which to rest her woman's heart, with all its caprices, and weaknesses, and capacity for love; perhaps she may have been even touched by the Tribune's unshaken devotion to herself, by the constancy which could withstand the allurements of vice, and even the distractions of political intrigue; perhaps to-day she disliked him less than on any former occasion, though it could hardly have been for *his* sake that her eye was heavy, and her bosom heaved. If so, whatever favour he had unconsciously gained, was as unconsciously destroyed by his own hand.

He approached her with an air of assumed confidence, that masked only too well the agitation of his real feelings.

"Fair Valeria," said he, "I have obeyed your commands, and I come like a faithful servant to claim my reward."

Now a woman's commands are not always intended to be literally obeyed. Under any circumstances she seldom likes to be reminded of them, and as for *claiming* anything from Valeria, why the very word roused all the rebellion that was dormant in her nature. At that instant rose on her mind's eye the scene in the amphitheatre, the level sand, the tossing sea of faces, the hoarse roar of the crowd, the strong white limbs and the yellow locks lying helpless beneath a dark vindictive face, and a glitter of uplifted steel. How she hated the conqueror then! How she hated him now!

She was clasping a bracelet carelessly on her arm, the fair round arm he admired so much, and that never looked so fair and round as in this gesture. It was part of his torture to make herself as attractive as she could.

Her cold eyes chilled him at once. "I had forgotten all about it," said she. "I am obliged to you for reminding me that I am in your debt."

Though somewhat hurt, he answered courteously. "There can be no debt from a mistress to her slave. You know, Valeria, that all of mine, even to my life, is at your disposal."

"Well?" she asked with a provoking persistency of misapprehension.

He began to lose his head, he, ordinarily so calm, and cunning, and self-reliant.

"You bade me enter on a difficult and dangerous undertaking. It was perhaps a lady's caprice, the merest possible whim. But you expressed a wish, and I never rested till I had accomplished it."

"You mean about that wretched slave," said she, and the colour rose faintly to her cheek. "But you never killed him after all."

How little he knew her! This then, he thought, was the cause of her coldness, of her displeasure. Esca had in some way incurred her ill-will, and she was angry with the conqueror who had spared him so foolishly when in his power. What a heart must this be of hers that could only quench its resentment in blood! Yet he loved her none the less. How the fair round arm and the stately head, and the turn of the white shoulder maddened him with a longing that was almost akin to rage. He caught her hand, and pressed it fervently to his lips.

"How can I please you?" he exclaimed, and his voice trembled with the only *real* emotion he perhaps had ever felt. "Oh! Valeria, you know that I love the very ground you tread on."

She bade Myrrhina bring her some embroidery on which the girl was busied, and thus effectually checked any further outpouring of sentiments which are not conveniently expressed within ear-shot of a third person. The waiting-maid took her seat at her mistress's elbow, her black eyes dancing in malicious mirth.

"Is that all you have to tell me?" resumed Valeria, with a smile in which coquetry, indifference, and conscious power were admirably blended. "Words are but empty air. My favour is reserved for those who win it by deeds."

"He shall die! I pledge you my word he shall die!" exclaimed the Tribune, still mis-understanding the beautiful enigma on which he had set his heart. "I have but spared him till I should know your pleasure, and now his fate is sealed. Ere this time to-morrow he will have crossed the Styx, and Valeria will repay me with one of her brightest smiles."

A shudder she could not suppress swept over the smooth white skin, but she suffered no trace of emotion to appear upon her countenance. She had a game to play now, and it must be played steadily and craftily to insure success. She bade Myrrhina fetch wine and fruit to place before her guest, and while the waiting-maid crossed the hall on her errand, she suffered the Tribune to take her hand once more, nay even returned its caressing clasp, with an almost imperceptible pressure. He was intoxicated with his success, he felt he was winning at last, and the jewelled cup that Myrrhina brought him, as he thought all too soon, remained for a while suspended in his hand, while he uttered fervent protestations of love, which were received with an equanimity that ought to have convinced him they were hopelessly wasted on his idol.

"You profess much," said she, "but it costs men little to promise. We have but one faithful lover in the empire, and he is enslaved by a barbarian princess and another man's wife. Would *you* have turned back from all the pleasures of Rome, to fight one more campaign against those dreadful Jews, for the sake of Berenice's sunburnt face?"

"Titus had consulted the oracle of Venus," replied the Tribune, with a meaning smile, "and doubtless the goddess had promised him a double victory. Valeria, you *know* there is nothing a man will not dare to win the woman he loves."

"Could *you* be as true?" she asked, throwing all the sweetness of her mellow voice, all the power of her winning eyes into the question.

"Try me," answered he, and for one moment the man's nature was changed, and he felt capable of devotion, self-sacrifice, fidelity, all that constitutes the heroism of love. The next, nature reasserted her sway, and he was counting the cost.

"I have a fancy for your barbarian," said Valeria carelessly, after a pause. "Myrrhina loves him, and—and if you will give him to me I will take him into my household."

Placidus shot a piercing glance at the waiting-maid, and that well-tutored damsel cast down her eyes and tried to blush. There was something, too, in Valeria's manner that did not satisfy him, and yet he was willing to believe more than he hoped, and nearly all he wished.

"I seldom *ask* for anything," resumed Valeria, raising her head with a proud, petulant gesture of which she knew the full effect. "It is far easier for me to grant a favour than to implore one.—And yet, I know not why, but I do not feel it painful to beg anything to-day from *you!*"

A soft smile broke over the haughty face while she spoke, and she raised her eyes and looked full into his for an instant, ere she lowered them to toy with the bracelet once more. It was the deadliest thrust she had in all her cunning of fence; the antagonist could seldom parry or withstand it; would it foil him in their present encounter? He loved her as much as such a nature *can* love, but the question was one of life and death, and it was no time for child's play now, as Esca was in possession of a secret that might annihilate his lord in an hour. The Tribune was not a man to sacrifice his very existence for a woman, even though that woman was Valeria. He hesitated, and she, marking his hesitation, turned pale, and shook with rage.

"You refuse me!" said she, in accents that

trembled either with suppressed fury or lacerated feelings. "You refuse me. *You*, the only man living for whom I would have so lowered myself. The only man I ever stooped to entreat. Oh! it is too much, too much."

She bowed her head in her hands, and as the wealth of brown hair showered over her white shoulders, they heaved as if she wept. Myrrhina looked reproachfully at the Tribune, and muttered, "Oh! if he knew, if he only *knew!*"

In his dealings with the other sex, Placidus had always been of opinion that it is better to untie a knot than to cut it. "Fair Valeria," said he, "ask me anything but this. I am pledged to slay this man within twenty-four hours—will not that content you?"

The exigency of the situation, the danger of him for whom she had conceived so wild and foolish a passion, sharpened her powers of deception, and made her reckless of her own feelings, her own degradation. Shaking the hair back from her temples, beautiful in her disorder and her tears, she looked with wet eyes in the Tribune's face, while she replied:

"Do you think I care for the barbarian? What difference can it make to Valeria if such as this

Briton were slain by hecatombs? It is for Myrrhina's sake I grieve, and more, far more than this, to think that you can refuse me anything in the whole world!"

Duplicity was no new effort for the Tribune. He had often, ere now, betaken himself to this mode of defence when driven to his last ward. He raised her hands respectfully to his lips. "Be it as you will," said he; "I make him over to you to do with him what you please. Esca is your property, beautiful Valeria, from this hour."

A dark thought had flitted through his brain, that it would be no such difficult matter to destroy an inconvenient witness, and retain the favour of an exacting mistress at the same time. It was but a grain or two of poison, in the slave's last meal, and he might depart in peace, a doomed man, to Valeria's mansion. He would take the chance of his silence for the few hours that intervened, and after all, the ravings of one whose brow was already stamped with death, would arouse little suspicion. Afterwards it would be easy to pacify Valeria, and shift the blame on some over-zealous freedman, or officious client. He did not calculate on the haste with which women jump to conclusions. Valeria clapped her hands with unusual glee. "Quick! Myrrhina," said she, "my tablets to the Tribune. He shall write the order here, and my people can go for the slave and bring him back, before Placidus departs."

"Nay," interposed the latter in some confusion; "it is indispensable that I go home at once. I have already lingered here too long. Farewell, Valeria. Ere the sun goes down, you shall see that Placidus is proud and happy to obey your lightest whim."

With these words, he made a low obeisance, and ere his hostess could stop him, had traversed the outer hall, and mounted in his chariot. Valeria seemed half-stupefied by this sudden departure, but ere the roll of his wheels had died away, a light gleamed in her eyes, and summoning the little negro who had lain unnoticed, and coiled up within call during the interview, she bade him run out and see which direction the chariot took, then she stared wildly in Myrrhina's face, and burst into a strange half-choking laugh.

CHAPTER III.

"FURENS QUID FŒMINA."

"THE chariot has turned into the Flaminian Way," said the urchin, running breathlessly back to his mistress. "Oh! so fast! so fast!" and he clapped his little black hands with the indescribable delight all children take in rapidity of movement.

"The Flaminian Way!" repeated Valeria. "He must go round by the Great Gate, and the Triumphal Arches, to get home. Myrrhina, if we make haste, we shall yet be in time."

In less than ten minutes, the two women had crossed the wide pleasure-grounds which skirted Valeria's mansion, and had let themselves out by a pass-key into the street. So complete, however, was their transformation that the most intimate friend would have failed to recognize in these shrouded, hurrying figures, the fashionable Roman lady and her attendant. A wig of curling yellow hair covered Valeria's nut-brown tresses, and the lower part of her face was concealed by a mask, whilst Myrrhina, closely veiled and wrapped in a dark-coloured mantle, stained and threadbare with many a winter's storm, looked like some honest child of poverty, bound on one of the humble errands of daily plebeian life.

As they tripped rapidly along a narrow and little frequented street, one of the many inconvenient thoroughfares which Nero's great fire had spared, and which still intersected the magnificence of the Imperial City, they had to pass a miserable-looking house, with a low shabby doorway which was yet secured by strong fastenings of bolts and bars, as though its tenant had sufficient motives for affecting privacy and retirement. The women looked meaningly at each other while they approached it, for the dwelling of Petosiris the Egyptian was too well known to all who led a life of pleasure or intrigue in Rome. He it was who provided potions, love-philtres, charms of every description, and whom the superstitious of all classes, no trifling majority, young and old, rich and poor, male and female, consulted in matters of interest and affection, the supplanting of a rival, the acquisition of a heart, and the removal of those who stood in the way either of a fortune or a conquest.

It is needless to observe that the Egyptian's wealth increased rapidly, and that humbler visitors had to turn from his door disappointed, day after day, waiting the leisure of the celebrated magician.

But if Valeria hurried breathlessly through the dirty and ill-conditioned street, she stopped transfixed when she reached its farthest extremity, and beheld the Tribune's chariot, standing empty in the shade, as though waiting for its master. The white horses beguiled their period of inaction in the heat, by stamping, snorting, and tossing their heads, while Automedon, now nodding drowsily, now staring vacantly about him, scarcely noticed the figures of the two women, so well were they disguised.

"What can he be doing there?" whispered Valeria, anxiously; and Myrrhina replied in the same cautious tones, "If Placidus be trafficking for philtres with the Egyptian, take my word for it, madam, there will be less of love than murder in the draught!"

Then they hurried on faster than before, as if life and death hung upon the rapidity of their footsteps.

Far back, up a narrow staircase, in a dark and secluded chamber, sat Petosiris, surrounded by the implements of his art. Enormous as his wealth was supposed to be, he suffered no symptoms of it to appear, either in his dwelling or his apparel. The walls of his chamber were bare and weather-stained, totally devoid of ornament, save for a mystic figure traced here and there on their surface, while the floor was scorched, and the ceiling blackened with the burning liquids that had fallen on the one, and the heavy aromatic vapours that clung about the other. The magician's own robe, though once of costly materials, and surrounded with a broad border, on which cabalistic signs and numerals were worked in golden thread, now sadly frayed, was worn to the last degree of tenuity, and his linen head-dress, wound in a multiplicity of folds, till it rose into a peak some two feet high, was yellow with dirt and neglect. Under this grotesque covering peered forth a pair of shrewd black eyes, set in a grave emaciated face. They denoted cunning, audacity, and that restless vigilance which argued some deficiency or warping of the brain, a tendency, however remote, to insanity, from which, with all their mental powers, these impostors are seldom free. There was nothing else remarkable about the man. He had the deep yellow tint with the supple figure and peculiar nostril of the Egyptian, and when he rose in compliment to his visitor, his low stature afforded a quaint contrast to his trailing robes, and real dignity of bearing.

The Tribune—for he it was whose entrance disturbed the calculations on which the magician was engaged—accosted the latter with an air of abrupt and almost contemptuous familiarity. It was evident that Placidus was a good customer, one who bought largely while he paid freely; and Petosiris, throwing aside all assumption of mystery or pre-occupation, laughed pleasantly as he returned the greeting. Yet was there something jarring in his laugh, something startling in his abrupt transition to the profoundest gravity; and though his small glittering eyes betrayed a schoolboy's love of mischief, gleams shot from them, at intervals, which expressed a diabolical malice, and love of evil for evil's sake.

"Despatch, my man of science!" said the

Tribune, scarcely noticing the obeisance, and expressions of regard lavished on him by his host. "As usual I have little time to spare, and less inclination to enter into particulars. Give me what I want, you have it here in abundance, and let me begone out of this atmosphere, which is enough to stifle the lungs of an honest man!"

"My lord! my illustrious patron! my worthiest friend!" replied the other with evident enjoyment of his customer's impatience, "you have but to command, you know it well, and I obey. Have I not served you faithfully in all my dealings? Was not the horoscope right to a minute? did not the charm protect from evil, and the love-philtre insure success? Have I ever failed, my noble employer?—speak, mighty Tribune, thy slave listens to obey."

"Words! words!" replied the other impatiently. "You know what I require. Produce it, there is the price!" At the same time he threw a bag of gold on the floor, the weight of which inferred that secresy must constitute no small portion of the bargain it was to purchase.

Though he affected utter unconsciousness, the Egyptian's eyes flashed at the welcome chink of the metal against the boards; none the more, however, would he abstain from tantalizing the donor by assuming a misapprehension of his meaning.

"The hour," said he, "is not propitious for casting a horoscope. Evil planets are in the ascendant, and the influence of the good genius is counteracted by antagonistic spells. Thus much I can tell you, noble Tribune, they are of barbarian origin. Come again an hour later, to-morrow, and I will do your bidding."

"Fool!" exclaimed Placidus, impatiently, at the same time raising his foot as though to spurn the magician like a dog. "Does a man give half a helmetful of gold for a few syllables of jargon scrawled on a bit of scorched parchment? You keep but one sort of wares that fetch a price like this. Let me have the strongest of them."

Neither the gesture, nor the insult it implied, were lost on the Egyptian. Yet he preserved a calm and imperturbable demeanour, while he continued his irritating inquiries.

"A philtre, noble patron? A love-philtre! They are indeed worth any amount of gold. Maid or matron, vestal virgin or Athenian courtesan, three drops of that clear tasteless fluid, and she is your own!"

The Tribune's evil smile was deepening round his mouth, it was not safe to jest with him any farther; he stooped over the magician and whispered two words in his ear; the latter looked up with an expression in which curiosity, horror, and a perverted kind of admiration were strangely blended.

Then his eyes twinkled once more with the schoolboy's mirth and malice, while he ransacked a massive ebony cabinet, and drew forth a tiny phial from its secret drawer. Wrapping this in a thin scroll, on which was written the word "*Cave*" (beware!) to denote the fatal nature of its contents, he hurried it into the Tribune's hands, hid away the bag of gold, and in a voice trembling with emotion, bade his visitor begone, an injunction which Placidus obeyed with his usual easy carelessness of demeanour, stepping daintily into his chariot, as though his errand had been of the most benevolent and harmless kind.

In the meantime, Valeria, accompanied by her attendant, had reached the Tribune's house, which she entered with a bold front indeed, but with shaking limbs. Despite her undaunted nature, all the fears and weaknesses of her sex were aroused by the task she had set herself to fulfil, and her woman's instinct told her that whatever might be her motives, the crossing of this notorious threshold was an act she would bitterly repent at some future time. Myrrhina entertained no such misgivings; she looked on the whole proceeding as an opportunity to display her own talents for intrigue, and make herself, if possible, more necessary than ever to the mistress, with whose secrets she was so dangerously familiar.

In the outer hall were lounging a few slaves and freedmen, who welcomed the entrance of the two women with considerably less respect than one of them at least was accustomed to consider her due. Damasippus indeed, with a coarse jest, strove to snatch away the mask that concealed the lower part of Valeria's face, but she released herself from his hold so energetically as to send him reeling back half a dozen paces, not a little discomfited by the unexpected strength of that shapely white arm. Then drawing herself to her full height, and throwing her disguise upon the floor, she confronted the astonished freed-man in her own person, and bade him stand out of her way.

"I am Valeria!" said she, "and here by your master's invitation, slave! for what are you better than a mere slave after all? If I were to hint at your insolence, he would have you tied to that door-post, in despite of your citizenship, and scourged to death, like a disobedient hound. Pick up those things," she added loftily, "and show me, some of you, to the private apartment of your lord. Myrrhina, you may remain outside, but within call."

Completely cowed by her demeanour, and no whit relishing the tone in which she threatened him, Damasippus did as he was commanded, while a couple of slaves who had remained till now in the background, ushered the visitor into another apartment, where they left her with many obsequious assurances that their lord was expected home every moment.

Every moment! Then there was no time to lose. How her heart beat, and what a strange instinct it was that made her feel she was in the vicinity of the man she loved! As yet she had formed no plan, she had made no determination, she only knew he was in danger, he was to die, and come what might, at any risk, at any sacrifice, her place was by his side. Imminent as was the peril, critical as was the moment, through all the tumult of her feelings, she was conscious of a vague wild happiness to be near him, and as she walked up and down the polished floor, counting its tessellated squares, mechanically, in her strong mental excitement, she pressed both hands hard against her bosom, as though to keep the heart within from beating so fiercely, and to collect all its energies by sheer strength and force of will.

Thus pacing to and fro, running over in her mind every possible and impossible scheme for the discovery and release of the slave, whose very prison she had yet to search out, her quick ear caught the dull and distant clank of a chain. The sound reached her from an opposite direction to that of the principal entrance; and as all Roman houses were constructed on nearly the same plan, Valeria had no fear of losing her way among the roomy halls and long corridors of her admirer's mansion. She held her breath as she hurried on, fortunately without meeting a human being, for the household slaves of both sexes had disposed themselves in shady nooks and corners to sleep away the sultriest hours of the day; nor did she stop till she reached a heavy crimson curtain, screening an inner court, paved and walled by slabs of white stone that refracted the sun's rays with painful intensity. Here she stood still and listened, while her very lips grew white with emotion, then she drew the curtain, and looked into the court.

He had dragged himself as far as his chain would permit, to get the benefit of some two feet of shade close under the stifling wall. A water-jar, long since emptied, stood on the floor beside him, accompanied by a crust of black, mouldy bread. A heavy iron collar, which defied alike strength and ingenuity, was round his throat, while the massive links that connected it with an iron staple let into the pavement would have held an elephant. It was obvious the prisoner could neither stand nor even sit upright without constraint; and the white skin of his neck and shoulders was already galled and blistered in his efforts to obtain relief by occasional change of posture. Without the key of the heavy padlock that fastened chain and collar, Vulcan himself could scarcely have released the Briton; and Valeria's heart sank within her as she gazed helplessly round, and thought of what little avail were her own delicate fingers for such a task. There seemed no nearer prospect of help even now that she had reached him; and she clenched her hand with anger while she reflected how he must have suffered from heat, and thirst, and physical pain, besides the sense of his degradation and the certainty of his doom.

Nevertheless, extended there upon the hard, glowing stones, Esca was sleeping as sound and peacefully as an infant. His head was pillowed on one massive arm, half hidden in the clustering yellow locks that showered across it, and his large shoulders rose and fell regularly with the measured breathing of a deep and dreamless slumber. She stole nearer softly, as afraid to wake him, and for a moment came upon Valeria's face something of the deep and holy tenderness with which a mother looks upon a child. Yet light as was that dainty footstep, it disturbed, without actually rousing, the watchful instincts of the sleeper. He stirred and turned his face upwards with a movement of impatience, while she, hanging over him and drinking in the beauty that had made such wild work with her tranquillity, as if her life had neither hope nor fear beyond the ecstasy of the moment, gazed on his fair features and his closed eyes, till she forgot time and place and hazard, the emergency of the occasion, and the errand on which she had herself come. Deeper and deeper sank into her being the dangerous influence of the hour and the situation. The summer sky above, the hot, dreamy solitude around, and there, down at her feet—nay, so near, that, while she bent over him, his warm breath stirred the very hair upon her brow—the only face of man that had ever thrilled her heart, sleeping so calmly close to her own, and now made doubly dear by all it had suffered, all it was fated to undergo. Lower and lower, nearer and nearer, bent her dainty head to meet the slave's; and as he stirred once more in his sleep, and a quiet smile stole over his unconscious countenance, her lips clung to his in one long, loving, and impassioned kiss.

CHAPTER IV.

THE LOVING CUP.

AS he opened his dreamy eyes she started to her feet, for voices now broke in on the silence that had hitherto reigned throughout the household, and the tread of slaves bustling to and fro announced the return of their lord, a master who brooked no neglect, as well they knew, from those who were in his service. She had scarcely risen from her posture of soothing and devoted affection—scarcely had time to shake the long hair off her face, when Julius Placidus entered the court and stood before her with that inscrutable expression of countenance which most she hated, and which left her in complete ignorance as to whether or not he had been in time to witness the caresses she had lavished on the captive. And now

Valeria vindicated the woman's nature of which, with all her faults, she partook so largely. At this critical moment her courage and presence of mind rose with the occasion; and though, woman-like, she had recourse to dissimulation, that refuge of the weak, there was something on her brow that argued, if need were, she would not shrink from the last desperate resources of the strong.

Turning to the Tribune with the quiet dignity and the playful smile that she knew became her so well, she pointed to the recumbent figure of the Briton, and said, gently—

"You gave him to me, and I am here to fetch him. Why is it that of late I value your lightest gift so much? Placidus, what must you think of me, to have come unbidden to your house?" Then she cast down her eyes and drooped her stately head, as though ready to sink in an agony of love and shame.

Deceiver, intriguer as he had been ever since the down was on his chin, he was no match for *her*. He shot, indeed, one sharp, inquisitive glance at Esca, but the slave's bewildered gaze reassured him. The latter, worn out with trouble and privation, was only half awake, and almost imagined himself in a dream. Then the Tribune's looks softened as they rested on his mistress; and, although there was a gleam of malicious triumph on his brow, the hard, unmeaning expression left his face, which brightened with more of kindness and cordiality than was its wont.

"It is no longer house of mine," said he, "but of yours, beautiful Valeria! Here you are ever welcome, and here you will remain, will you not, with him who loves you better than all the world besides?"

Even while he spoke she had run over in her mind the exigencies and difficulties of her position. In that instant of time she could think of Esca's danger, of the necessity that she should herself be present to save him from the fate with which, for some special reason, that she was also determined to find out, he was obviously threatened; of the Tribune's infamous character, and her own fair fame, for Cornelia might not have left such a house as that with her reputation unscathed, and Valeria could far less afford to tamper with so fragile and shadowy a possession than the severe mother of the Gracchi. Yet her brow was unclouded, and there was nothing but frank good-humour in her tone while she replied—

"Nay, Placidus. You know that even we of

the patrician order cannot do always as we would. Surely I have risked enough already; because—because I fancied you left me in anger, and I could not bear the thought even for an hour. I will but ask you for a cup of wine, and begone. Myrrhina accompanied me here, and we can return unknown and unsuspected as we came."

He wished nothing better. A cup of wine, a sumptuous feast spread on the moment, garlands of flowers, heavy perfumes loading the sultry air, soft music stealing on the senses gently as the faint breeze that whispered through the drowsy shade. All the voluptuous accessories so adapted to a pleading tongue and so dangerous to a willing ear. He had never known them fail: it should not be the fault of master or household if they proved useless now.

He took Valeria respectfully by the hand, and led her to the large banqueting-hall with as much deference as though she had been Cæsar's wife. None knew better than the Tribune how scrupulously all the honours of war must be paid to a fortress about to capitulate. As he bent before her, the phial he had purchased from Petosiris peeped forth in the bosom of his tunic, and her quick eye did not fail to detect it. In an instant she turned back as though stumbling on the skirt of her robe, and in the action made a rapid sign to Esca by raising her hand to her mouth, accompanied by a warning shake of the head and a glance from her eloquent eyes, that she trusted he would understand as forbidding him to taste either food or drink till her return. Once more, whilst she made this covert signal, the set and passionless look came over the Tribune's face. Cunning, cautious as she might think herself, his snake-like eye had seen enough. At that moment Placidus had resolved Esca should die within the hour. Then those two walked gracefully into the adjoining hall, and seated themselves at the banquet with a scrupulous courtesy and strict observance of the outward forms of good breeding, while the slaves who waited believed that the whole proceeding was but one of their lord's usual affairs of gallantry, and that the noble pair before them loved each other well.

The Tribune, like the rest of his sex, was no large eater when making love; and an appetite that could accompany Vitellius through the most elaborate banquets of the gluttonous Cæsar was satisfied with a handful of dates and a bunch or two of grapes in the presence of Valeria. She, too, in her anxiety and agitation, felt as if every morsel would choke her; but she pledged her host willingly in a goblet of red Falernian, with a vague idea that every moment she could keep his attention employed was of priceless value, clinging almost hopelessly to the chance of obtaining by some means the possession of the fatal phial before it was too late.

He was in high spirits,—voluble, witty, eloquent, sarcastic, but devoted to her. In the moment, as he hoped, of his triumph he could afford to show, or rather to affect, more of delicacy and generosity than she had believed him to possess, and she loathed and hated him all the more. Once, when, after enunciating a sentiment of the warmest regard and attachment, she caught the expression of his eyes as they looked into her own, she glanced wildly round the room, and clenched her hand with rage to observe that the walls were bare of weapons. He was no stately, high-spirited Agamemnon, this supple intriguer, yet had there been sword, axe, or dagger within reach of that white arm, she would have asked nothing better than to enact the part of Clytemnestra. How she wished for the moment to be a man—ay, and a strong one! She felt she could have strangled him there, hateful and smiling, on the couch! Oh! for Esca's thews and sinews! Esca—so fair, and brave, and honest! Her brain swam when she thought of him chained, like a beast, within ten paces of her. An effort must be made to save him at any risk and at any sacrifice.

Placidus talked gaily on, broaching in turn those topics of luxury, dissipation, and even vice, which constituted the every-day life of the patrician order at Rome, and she forced herself to reply with an affected levity and indifference that nearly drove her mad. Cæsar's banquets; Galeria's yellow head-gear, and the bad taste in which her jewels were set, so inexcusable in an Emperor's wife; the war in Judæa; the last chariot-race; and the rival merits of the Red and Green factions, were canvassed and dismissed with a light word and a happy jest. Such subjects inevitably led to a discussion on the arena and its combatants, the magnificence of the late exhibition, and the Tribune's own prowess in the deadly game. Placidus turned suddenly, as if recollecting himself, called for a slave, whispered an order in his ear, and bade him begone. The man hastened from the room, leaving lover and mistress once more alone.

The presence of mind and self-command on which she prided herself now completely deserted Valeria. In an agony of alarm for Esca, she jumped at once to the conclusion that his doom was gone forth. The Tribune, turning to her with some choice phrase, half jest, half compliment, was startled to observe her face colourless to the very lips, while her large eyes shone with a fierce, unnatural light. Uttering a low, stifled cry, like that of some wild animal in its death-pang, she fell at his feet, clasping him round the knees, and gasped out—

"Spare him! spare him! Placidus—beloved Placidus! spare him—for *my* sake!"

Her host, whose whole mind at that moment was occupied with thoughts very foreign to bloodshed, and whose whispered mandate had reference to nothing more deadly than orders for a strain of unexpected music, gazed in astonishment at the proud woman thus humbled before him to the dust. He had, indeed, intended to despatch Esca quietly by poison before nightfall, and so get rid at once of an inconvenient witness and a possible rival; but for the present he had dismissed the slave completely from his mind. If, an hour ago, he had allowed himself to harbour such a wild fancy, as that a mere barbarian should have captivated the woman on whom he had set his affections, her voluntary acceptance of his hospitality and her cordial demeanour since, had dispelled so foolish and unjust a suspicion, which he wondered he could have entertained even for a moment.

Now, however, a chill seemed to curdle the blood about his heart. Very quietly he raised her from the floor; but, though he was not conscious of it, his grasp left a mark upon her wrist. Very distinct and steady were the tones in which he soothed her, asking courteously—

"Whom do you wish me to spare? What is it, Valeria? Surely you are not still dwelling on that barbarian slave? What is he, to come between you and me? It is too late—too late!"

"Never! never!" she gasped out, seizing his hand in both her own, and folding it to her breast. "It is no time now for concealment; no time for choice phrases, and mock reserve, and false shame! I love him, Placidus! I love him!—do you hear? Grant me but his life, and ask me for everything I have in return!"

She looked beautiful as she knelt before him once more, so dishevelled and disordered, with upturned face and streaming hair. It seemed to the Tribune as though a knife had been driven home to his heart; but he collected all his energies for a revenge commensurate to the hurt, as he threw himself indolently on the couch, a worse man by a whole age of malice than he had risen from it a few seconds before.

"Why did you not tell me sooner?" said he, in accents of the calmest courtesy and self-command. "Fair Valeria! not more bargains are driven every day in the Forum than in the courts of Love! You offer liberal terms. It seems to me we have nothing left to do but to settle the remainder of the agreement."

What a price was she paying for her interference! Not a woman in Rome could have felt more deeply the degradation she was accepting —the insult to which she was submitting, and through it all she was miserably conscious of a false move in the game she had the temerity to play against this formidable adversary. Still she had resolved that she would shrink from no humiliation to save Esca, and she blushed blood-red with anger and shame as she rose from her knees, hid her face in her hands, while she summoned her woman's wit and her woman's powers of endurance to help her in the emergency.

He, too, had bethought him of an appropriate revenge. The Tribune never forgave; for such an offence as the present it was his nature to seek reprisals, exceeding, in their subtle cruelty, the injury they were to atone. There is no venom so deadly as a bad man's love turned to gall. It would be fine sport, thought Placidus, to make her slay this yellow-haired darling of hers, with her own hand. The triumph would be complete, when he had outwitted her at every point, and could sneer politely over the dead body of the man, and the passionate reproaches of the woman. The first step to so tempting a consummation was, of course, to put her off her guard, and for this it would be necessary to assume some natural displeasure and pique; too open a brow would surely arouse suspicions, so he spoke angrily, in the harsh, excited tones of a generous man who has been wronged.

"I have been deceived," said he, striking his hand against the board; "deceived, duped, scorned, and by *you*, Valeria, from whom I did not deserve it. Shame on the woman who could thus wring an honest heart for the mere triumph of her vanity. And yet," he added, with an admirable appearance of wounded feeling in his lowered voice and relenting accents, "I can forgive, because I would not others should suffer as I do now. Yes, Valeria's wishes are still laws to me: I *will* spare him for your sake, and you shall bear the news to him yourself. But he must be half dead ere this, of thirst and exhaustion; take him a cup of wine with your own fair hands, and tell him he will be a free man before sunset!"

While he spoke, he turned from her to a sideboard, on which stood a tall jar of Falernian, flanked by a pair of silver goblets. She had sunk from the couch beside him, and was resting her head upon the table; but she looked up quickly for a moment, and saw his back reflected in the burnished surface of a gold vase that stood before her. By the motion of his shoulders she was aware that he had taken something from his bosom while he filled the wine. The whole danger of the situation flashed upon her at once; she felt intuitively that one of the cups was poisoned; she could risk her life to find out which. Her tears were dried, her nerves were strung, as if by magic: like a different being she rose to her feet now, pale and beautiful, but perfectly calm and composed.

"You *do* love me, Placidus," said she, raising

one of the goblets from the salver on which they stood. "Such truth as yours might win any woman. I pledge you to show that we are friends again at least, if nothing more!"

She was in the act of putting it to her lips, when he interposed, somewhat hurriedly, and with a voice not so steady as usual—

"One moment!" he exclaimed, taking it from her hand, and setting it down again in its place, "we have not made our terms yet; the treaty must be signed and sealed; a libation must be poured to the gods. It is a strong rough wine, that Falernian, I have some Coan here you would like better. You see I have not forgotten your tastes."

He laughed nervously, and his lip twitched; she knew now that it was the right-hand goblet which held the poison. Both were equally full, and they stood close together on the salver.

"And this man could not slay me after all," was the thought that for a moment softened her heart, and bade her acknowledge some shadow of compunction for her admirer. Bad as he was she could not help reflecting that to her influence he owed the only real feeling his life had ever known, and it made her waver, but not for long.

Soon the image of Esca, chained and prostrate, passed before her, and the remembrance of her odious bargain goaded her into the bitterest hatred once more.

She placed her hand in the Tribune's with the abandonment of a woman who really loves, she turned her eyes on his with the swimming glance of which she had not miscalculated the power.

"Forgive me," she murmured. "I have never valued you, never known you till now. I was heartless, unfeeling, mad; but I have learned a lesson to-day that neither of us will ever forget. No, we will never quarrel again!"

He clasped her in his arms, he took her to his heart, his brain reeled, his senses failed him, that bewitching beauty seemed to pervade his being, to surround him with its fragrance like some intoxicating vapour; and whilst his frame thrilled, and his lips murmured out broken words of fondness, the white hand thrown so confidingly across his shoulder had shifted the position of the goblets, and the heart that beat so wildly against his own, had doomed him remorselessly to die.

She extricated herself from his embrace, she

put her hair back from her brow; love is blind, indeed, or it must have struck him that instead of blushing with conscious fondness, her cheek was as white and cold as marble, though she kept her eyes cast down as if they dared not meet his own.

"Pledge me," said she, in a tone of the utmost softness, and forcing a playful smile that remained, carved as it were, in fixed lines round her mouth. "Drink to me in token of forgiveness; it will be the sweetest draught I have ever tasted when your lips have kissed the cup."

He reached his hand out gaily to the salver. Her heart stood still in the agony of her suspense, lest he should mark the change she had made so warily; but the goblets were exactly alike, and he seized the nearest without hesitation, and half-emptied it ere he set it down. Laughing, he was in act of handing to her what remained, when his eye grew dull, his jaw dropped, and stammering some broken syllables, he sank back senseless upon the couch.

She would have almost given Esca's life now to undo the deed. But it was no time for repentance or indecision; keeping her eyes off the white vacant face, which yet seemed ever before her, she felt resolutely in the bosom of the Tribune's tunic for the precious key, and having found it, walked steadily to the door and listened. It was well she did so, for a slave's step was heard rapidly approaching, and she had but time to return, on tiptoe, and take her place upon the couch ere the domestic entered; disposing of the Tribune's powerless head upon her lap as though he had sunk to sleep in her embrace. The slave discreetly retired, but short as was its duration, the torture of those few seconds was hardly inadequate to the guilt that had preceded them. Then she hurried through the well-known passages, and reached the court in which Esca was confined. Not a word of explanation, not a syllable of fondness escaped her lips as she calmly liberated the man for whom she had risked so much.

Mechanically, and like a sleep-walker, she unlocked the collar round his neck, signing to him at the same time, for she seemed incapable of speech, to rise and follow her. He obeyed, scarce knowing what he did, astonished at the apparition of his deliverer, and almost scared by her ghastly looks, and strange imperious gestures. Thus they threaded, without interruption, the passages of the house, and emerged from the private entrance into the now silent and deserted street. Then came the reaction: Valeria could bear up no longer, and trembling all over, while she clung to Esca, but for whose arm she must have fallen, she burst into a passion of sobs upon his breast.

CHAPTER V.

SURGIT AMARI.

SHE had known but few moments of happiness, that proud, unbending woman, in the course of her artificial life. Now, though remorse was gnawing at her heart, there was such a wild delight in the Briton's presence, such ecstasy in the consciousness of having saved him, though at the price of a hateful crime, that the pleasure kept down and stifled the pain. It was a new sensation to cling to that stalwart form and acknowledge him for her lord whom others deemed a mere barbarian and a slave. It was intense joy to think that *she* had penetrated his noble character, that *she* had given him her love unasked, when such a gift could alone have saved him from destruction, and that *she* had grudged no price at which to ransom him for herself. It was the first time in Valeria's whole existence that she had indicated her woman's birthright of merging her own existence in another's, and for the moment this engrossing consciousness completely altered the whole character and training of the Patrician lady. Myrrhina walking discreetly some ten paces behind, could hardly believe in the identity of that drooping form, faltering in step, and timid in gesture, with her imperious and wilful mistress.

This vigilant damsel, who was never flurried or surprised, had effected her escape from the domestics of the Tribune's household, at the moment her practised ear caught the light footstep of Valeria making its way to the door; and although she scarcely expected to see the latter pacing home with the captive at her side, as oblivious of her waiting-maid's existence, as of everything else in the world, she was quite satisfied to observe that this preoccupation was the result of interest in her companion. So long as an intrigue was on foot, it mattered little to Myrrhina who might be its originators or its victims.

They had not proceeded far before Esca stopped, waking up like a man from a dream.

"I owe you my life," he said, in his calm voice and foreign accent that made such music to her ear. "How shall I ever repay you, noble lady? I have nothing to give but the strength of my right arm, and of what service can such as I be to such as you?"

She blushed deeply, and cast down her eyes—"We are not safe yet," she answered. "We will talk of this when we get home."

He looked before him down the stately street, with its majestic porticoes, its towering palaces, and its rows of lofty pillars, stretching on in grand perspective till they met the dusky crimson of the evening sky, and perhaps he was thinking of a free upland, and blue hills, and laughing sunshine glittering on the mere and trembling in the green wood far away at home, for he only answered by repeating her last word with a sigh, and adding—"There is none for me; a wanderer, an outcast, and a degraded man."

She seemed to check the outburst that was rising to her lips, and she kept her eyes off his face, while she whispered—

"I have determined to save you. Do you not know that there is nothing you can ask me which I will not grant?"

He raised her hand to his lips, but the gesture partook more of the dependent's homage than the lover's rapture. She felt instinctively that it was a tribute of gratitude and loyalty, not an impassioned caress. For the second time, something seemed to warn her she had better have left that day's work undone. Then she began to talk rapidly of the dangers they might undergo from pursuit, of the necessity for immediate flight to her house, and close concealment when there, wandering wildly on from one subject to another, and, apparently, but half-conscious of anything she said.

At last he asked her eagerly, even sternly;—"And the Tribune? What of him? How could you release me from his power? I tell you, I had the life of Placidus in my hand, as completely as if I had been standing over him in the Amphitheatre with my foot on his neck. Would *any* price have purchased me from him, with all I knew?"

The crimson rose to her brow, as she answered hurriedly—"No price! Believe me, no price that man could offer, or woman either! Esca, do not think worse of me than I deserve!"

"Then why am I here?" he continued, with a

softened look. "I would like well to discover the secret by which Valeria can charm such a man as Placidus to her will."

She was very pale now. "The Tribune will claim you no more," said she; "I have settled that account for ever."

He did not understand her, yet he dropped the hand he held and walked on a little further from her side. She felt her punishment had already commenced, and when she spoke again it was in hard cold accents quite unlike her own.

"He crossed my path, Esca, and he met the fate of all who are rash enough to oppose Valeria. What motives of pity, or love, or honour, would avail with Placidus? When did he ever swerve a hair's-breadth from his goal for any consideration but self? I knew him, ah! too well. There was but one invincible argument for the Tribune, and I used it. I slew him; slew him there, upon his couch; but it was to save *you!*"

Perhaps he felt he was ungrateful. Perhaps he tried to think that he, at least, had no right to judge her harshly; that such devotion for *his* sake should have made him look with indulgent eye, even on so foul a crime as murder; but he could not control the repugnance and horror that now rose in him for this beautiful, reckless, and unscrupulous woman; but while he strove to conceal his feelings, and to mask them with an air of deference and gratitude, she knew by the instinct of love all that was passing in his breast, and suffered, as those only *can* suffer, who have thrown honour, virtue, conscience, everything to the winds, to purchase but the conviction that their shameful sacrifice has been in vain.

She determined to put a period to the tortures she was enduring. Ere this, they had reached the street, from which opened the private entrance into her own grounds. Myrrhina, though within sight, still kept discreetly in the rear. This was the situation, this was the moment that Valeria had pictured to herself in many a rapturous day-dream, that seemed too impossibly happy ever to come to pass. To have ransomed him from some great danger at some equivalent price; to have led him off with her in triumph; those two pacing by themselves through the deserted streets at the witching sunset hour; to have brought him home her own, her very own, to this identical gate exactly in this manner; to have none between them, none to watch them except faithful Myrrhina, and to see before her a long future of uninterrupted sunshine, this it had been ecstacy to dream of—and now it had come, and brought with it a dull, sickening sensation that was worse than pain.

She had a brave rebellious nature, in keeping with the haughty head and stately form hereditary in her line. No scion of that noble old house would shrink or quiver under mental, any more than under bodily torture. Among the ancestral busts that graced her cornices, was that of one who endured with a calm set face to watch his own hand shrivelled up and crackling in the glowing coals. His descendants, male and female, partook of that unflinching character, and not Mutius Scævola himself, erect and stern before the Tuscan king, had more of the desperate tenacity which sets fate itself at defiance, than lurked under the soft white skin, and the ready smile, and the voluptuous beauty of proud Valeria.

She looked prouder and fairer than ever now, as she stopped at her own gate, and confronted the Briton.

"You are safe," she said, and what it cost her to say it, none knew but herself. "You are free besides, and at liberty to go where you will."

The rapture with which he kissed her hand

while she spoke, the gleam of delight that lit up his whole face, the intense gratitude with which he bowed himself to the ground before her, smote like repeated strokes of a dagger to her heart.

She continued in accents of well-acted indifference, though a less preoccupied observer might have marked the quivering eyelid and dilated nostril. "You may have friends whom you long to see—friends who have been anxious about your safety. Though it seems," she added ironically, "they have taken but little pains to set you out of danger."

Esca was always frank and honest; this was perhaps the charm that, combined with his yellow locks and broad shoulders, so endeared him to the Roman lady. She was unaccustomed to these qualities in the men she usually met.

"I have no friends," he answered rather sadly. "None in the whole of this great city, except perhaps yourself, noble lady, who care whether I am alive or dead. Yet I have one mission, for the power of performing which this very night I thank you far more than for saving my life. To-morrow, it would be too late."

The tone was less that of a question than an assertion, in which she forced out the words—

"It concerns that dark-eyed girl!—Esca, do not fear to tell me the truth."

A faint red stole over the young man's brow. They were standing together within the garden-wall on the smooth lawn that sloped towards the house. The black cedars cut clear and distinct against the pure serene opal of the fading sky. A star or two were dimly visible, and not a breath stirred the silent foliage of the holm-oaks, folded, as it were, in sleep, or the drooping flowers, drowsy with the very weight of fragrance they exhaled. It was the time and place for a confession of love. What a mockery it seemed to Valeria to stand there and watch his rising colour, and listen to the faltering voice in which he betrayed his secret!

"I must save her, noble lady," said he; "I must save her this very night, whatever else be left undone. Be he dead or alive, she shall not enter the Tribune's house, whilst I can strike a blow or grasp an enemy by the throat. Lady, you have earned my eternal gratitude, my eternal service; give me but this one night, and I return to-morrow to be the humblest and most willing of your slaves for ever after."

"And see her no more?" asked Valeria, with

a choking throat and a strong tendency to burst into tears.

"And see her no more," repeated Esca, sadly and resignedly. There was no mistaking the tone of manly, unselfish, and utterly hopeless love.

Valeria passed her hand across her face, and tried more than once to speak. At last she muttered in a hoarse hard voice—

"You love her then very dearly?"

He raised his head proudly, and a smile came on his lips, a light into his blue eyes. She remembered how he had looked so in the arena, when he gave his salute before the Imperial chair. She remembered too a pair of dark eyes, and a pale face, that followed his every movement.

"So dearly," was his answer, "that can I but rescue her, I will gladly bargain to give her up and never even look on her again. How can I think of myself when the question is of *her* happiness and *her* safety?"

Valeria with all her faults was a woman. She had indeed dreamed of an affection such as this, an affection purified from the dross and alloy that combines to form so much of what men call love.

She might not be capable of feeling it, but womanlike, she could admire and appreciate the nobility of its aspirations, and the ideal standard to which it stretched. Womanlike too, she was not to be outdone in generosity, and Esca's proposal of returning to her household, and submitting to her will directly he had accomplished his errand, disarmed her completely. She was not accustomed to analyze her feelings, or to check the reckless impulse which always bade her act on the spur of the moment. She did not stop to consider to-morrow's repentance, nor the grudging regrets which would goad her when the excitement of her self-denial had died out, and the blank that had hitherto rendered existence so dreary would be even less tolerable than before. If a shadowy misgiving that she would repent her concession hereafter, passed for a moment across her mind, she hastened to repress it, ere it should warp her better intentions; and she could urge him to leave her now, with all the more importunity, that she dared not trust her heart to waver for an instant in the sacrifice.

"You are alone," said she, calming herself with a great effort, and speaking very quick. "Alone in this great city, but you are loyal and brave.

Such men are rare here and are worth a legion. Still, you must have gold in your bosom and steel at your belt, if you would succeed. You shall take both from me, and you will tell the dark-eyed girl that it was Valeria who saved her and you." His blue eyes turned upon her with looks of the deepest, the most fervent gratitude, and again the wild love surged up in her heart, and threatened to swamp every consideration but its own irresistible longing. His answer, however, sent it ebbing coldly back again.

"We shall be ever grateful—oh! that either of us could prove it! We shall not forget Valeria."

Myrrhina thought her mistress had never looked so queenly, as when she called her up at this juncture, and bade her fetch a purse of gold from her own cabinet, and one of the swords that hung in the vestibule, and deliver them to Esca. Then, very erect and pale, Valeria walked towards the house, apparently insensible to his thanks and protestations, but turned round ere she had reached the threshold, and gave him her hand to kiss. Myrrhina returning from her errand, saw the face that was bent over him as he stooped in act of homage, and even that hollow-hearted girl was touched by its wild, tender, and mournful expression, but ere he could look up, it was cold and passionless as marble, once more. Then she disappeared slowly through the porch, and Myrrhina with all her daring had not the courage to follow her into the privacy of her own chamber.

CHAPTER VI.

"DEAD LEAVES."

THE stars shone brilliantly down on the roofs of the great city—roofs that covered in how various a multitude of hopes, fears, wishes, crimes, joys, study, debaucheries, toil, and repose. What enormities were veiled by a tile some half an inch thick! What contrasts separated by a partition of a deal plank, and a crevice stopped with mortar! Here, a poor worn son of toil, working with bleared eyes, and hollow cheeks to complete the pittance that a whole day's labour was insufficient to attain; there a sleek pampered slave, snoring greasily on his pallet, drenched with pilfered wine, and gorged with the fat leavings of his master's meal. On this side the street, a whole family penned helplessly together in a stifling garret, on that a spacious palace, with marble floors, and airy halls, and lofty corridors, devoted to the occasional convenience and the shameful pleasures of one man—a patrician in rank, a senator in office; yet, notwithstanding a profligate, a coward, a traitor, and a debauchee. Could those roofs have been taken off, could those chambers have been bared to the million eyes of night that seemed to be watching her so intently, what a mass of corruption would Imperial Rome have laid bare! There were plague spots under her purple, festering and spreading and eating into the very marrow of the Mistress of the world. Up six stories, under the slanting roof, in a miserable garret, a scene was being enacted, bad as it was, far below the nightly average of vice and treachery in Rome.

Dismissed from their patron's house when he had no further need of their attendance, and so to speak, off duty for the day, Damasippus and Oarses had betaken themselves to their home in order to prepare for the exploits of the night. That home was of the cheapest and most wretched among the many cheap and wretched lodgings to be found in the overgrown yet crowded city. Four bare walls bulging and blistered with the heat, supported the naked rafters on which rested the tiles, yet glowing from an afternoon sun. A wooden bedstead, rickety and creaking, with a coarse pallet, through the rents of which the straw peeped and rustled, occupied one corner, and a broken jar of common earthenware but of a sightly design copied from the Greek, half-full of tepid water, stood in another. These constituted the only furniture of the apartment, except a few irregular shelves filled with unguents, cosmetics, and the inevitable pumice-stone, by which the fashionable Roman studied to eradicate every superfluous hair from his unmanly cheek and limbs. A broken Chiron, in common plaster, yet showing marks of undoubted genius, where the shoulders and hoofs of the Centaur had escaped mutilation, kept guard over these treasures, and filled a place that in the pious days of the old Republic, however humble the dwelling, would have been occupied by the Lares and Penates of the hearth. A mouldy crust of bread slipped from the lid of an open trunk full of clothing, lay on the floor, and a jar of wine emptied to the dregs stood by its side.

The two inhabitants, however, of this squalid apartment betrayed in their persons none of the misery in keeping with their dwelling-place. They were tolerably well-fed because their meals were usually furnished at their patron's expense; they contrived to be well-dressed, because a decent and even wealthy appearance was creditable to their patron's generosity, and indispensable to many of the duties he called upon them to perform, dirty work indeed, but only to be done, nevertheless, with clean clothes and an assured countenance, so that the exterior both of Damasippus and Oarses would have offered no discredit to the anteroom of Cæsar himself. But they were men of pleasure, as the word is understood in great cities, men who lived solely for the sensual indulgences of the body; and it was their nature to spend their gains, chiefly ill-gotten, in those debasing luxuries, which an insatiable demand enabled Rome to supply to her public, at the lowest possible cost, to sun themselves as it were, in the glare of that gaudy vice, which walks abroad in the streets, and then creep back into their loathsome hole, like reptiles as they were.

Damasippus, whose plump, well-rounded form and clear colour afforded a remarkable contrast to the lithe shape and sallow tint of Oarses, was the first to speak. He had been watching the Egyptian intently, while the latter went through the painful and elaborate ceremonies of a protracted toilet, rasping his chin with the pumice-stone, smoothing and greasing his dark locks with a preparation of lard and perfumed oil, and finally drawing a needle charged with lamp-black, carefully and painfully through his closed eyelids, in order to lengthen the line of the eye, and give it that soft languishing expression so prized by Orientals of either sex. Damasippus waxing impatient then, at the evident satisfaction with which his friend pursued the task of adornment, broke out irritably—

"And of course it is to be the old story again! As usual, mine the trouble, and by Hercules no small share of the danger, now that the town is swarming with soldiers, all discontented and ill-paid. While yours, the credit, and very likely the reward, and nothing to do but to whine out a few coaxing syllables, and make yourself as like an old woman as you can. No difficult task either," he added, with a half-sarcastic, half-good-humoured laugh.

The other lingered before a few inches of cracked mirror, which seemed to rivet his attention, and put the finishing touches to either eyelid with infinite care, ere he replied:

"Every tool to its own work, and every man to his special trade. The wooden-headed mallet to drive home the sharp wedge. The brute force of Damasippus to support the fine skill of Oarses."

"And the sword of a Roman," retorted the other, who, like many untried men, was somewhat boastful of his mettle, "to hew a path for the needlework of an Egyptian. Well, at least the needle is in appropriate hands. By all the fountains of Caria thou hast the true feminine leer in thine eye, the very swing of thy draperies seems to say 'Follow me, but not too near.' The clasp of Salmacis herself could not have effected a more perfect transformation: Oarses, thou lookest an ugly old woman to the life!"

In truth the Egyptian's disguise was now nearly complete. The dark locks smoothed and flattened were laid in modest bands about his head—the matronly stole, or gown, gathered at the breast by a broad girdle, and fastened with a handsome clasp high on the shoulder, descended in long sweeping lines to his feet, where it was ornamented by a broad and elaborate flounce of embroidery. Over the whole was disposed in graceful folds a large square shawl of the finest texture, dark-coloured but woven through with glistening golden threads and further set off by a wide golden fringe. It formed a veil and cloak in one, and might easily be arranged to conceal the figure as well as the face of the wearer. Oarses was not a little proud of the dainty feminine grace with which he wore the head-gear, and as he tripped to and fro across the narrow floor of his garret, it would have taken a sharper eye than that of keen Damasippus himself to detect the disguise of his wily confederate.

"A woman, my friend," he replied, somewhat testily, "but not such an *ugly* one, after all; as thou wilt find to thy cost when we betake ourselves to the streets. I look to thee, my Damasippus," he added maliciously, "to protect thy fair companion from annoyance and insult."

Damasippus was a coward and he knew it, so he answered stoutly—

"Let them come, let them come! a dozen at a time, if they will. What! a good blade and a light helmet is enough for me, though you put me at half-sword with a whole maniple of gladiators! The patron knows what manhood is, none better. Why should he have selected Damasippus for this enterprise, but that he judges my arm is iron, and my heart is oak?"

"And thy forehead brass," added the Egyptian, scarcely concealing a contemptuous smile.

"And my forehead brass," repeated the other, obviously gratified by the compliment. "Nay, friend, the shrinking heart, and the failing arm, and the womanly bearing, are no disgrace, perhaps, to a man born by the tepid Nile; but we who drink from the Tiber here (and very foul it is)—we of the blood of Romulus, the she-wolf's litter, and the war-god's line—are never so happy as when our feet are reeling in the press of battle, our hearts leaping to the clash of shields, and our ears deafened by the shout of victory. Hark! what is that?"

The boaster's face turned very pale, and he hastily unbuckled the sword he had been girding on while he spoke, for a wild, ominous cry came sweeping over the roofs of the adjoining houses, rising and falling, as it seemed, with the sway of deadly strife, and boding in its fierce fluctuations, to some a cruel triumph, to others a merciless defeat.

Oarses heard it too. His dark face scarce looked like a woman's now, with its gleam of malicious glee, and exulting cunning.

"The old Prætorians are up," said he, quietly.

"I have been expecting this for a week. Brave soldier, there will be a fill of fighting for thee this night in the streets, and goodly spoils, too, for the ready hand, and love and wine, and all the rest of it, without the outlay of a farthing."

"But it will not be safe to be seen in arms now," gasped Damasippus, sitting down on the tester-bed, with a white, flabby face, and a general appearance of being totally unstrung. "Besides," he added, with a ludicrous attempt at reasserting his dignity, "a brave Roman should not engage in civil war."

Oarses reflected for a moment, undisturbed by a second shout, that made his frightened companion tremble in every limb, then he smoothed his brows, and spoke in soothing and persuasive tones.

"Dost thou not see, my friend, how all is in favour of our undertaking? Had the city been quiet, we might have aroüsed attention, and a dozen chance passengers half as brave as thyself, might have foiled us at the very moment of success. Now, the streets will be clear of small parties, and it is easy for us to avoid a large body before it approaches. One act of violence amongst the hundreds sure to be committed to-night, will never again be heard of. The three or four resolute slaves under thine orders, will be taken to belong to one or other of the fighting factions, and thus even the patron's spotless character will escape without a blemish. Besides, in such a turmoil as we are like to have by sundown, a woman might scream her heart out, and nobody would think of noticing her. On with that sword again, my hero, and let us go softly down into the street."

"But if the Old Prætorians succeed," urged the other, evincing a great disinclination for the adventure, "what will become of Cæsar? and with Cæsar's fall, down goes the patron too, and then who is to bear us harmless from the effects of our expedition to-night?"

"Oh! thick-witted Ajax!" answered the Egyptian, laughing. "Bold and strong in action as the lion; but in counsel innocent as the lamb. Knowest thou the Tribune so little as to think he will be on the losing side? If there is tumult in Rome, and revolt, and the city boils and seethes like a huge flesh-pot casting up its choicest morsels to the surface, dost thou suppose that Placidus is not stirring the fire underneath? I tell thee that come what may of Cæsar to-night, to-morrow will behold the Tribune more popular and more powerful than ever; and I for one will beware of disobeying his behests."

The last argument was not without its effect, Damasippus, though much against the grain, was persuaded that of two perils, he had better choose the least; and it speaks well for the ascendancy gained by Placidus over his followers, that the cleverer and more daring knave should have obeyed him unhesitatingly from self-interest, the ruffian and the coward from fear. Damasippus, then, girding on his sword once more, and assuming as warlike a port as was compatible with his sinking heart, marched down into the street to accompany his disguised companion on their nefarious undertaking, with many personal fears and misgivings for the result.

How different, save in its disquietude, was the noble nature, at the same moment seeking repose and finding none, within half a bow-shot of the garret in which these two knaves were plotting. Despite his blameless life, despite his distinguished career, Caius L. Licinius sat and brooded, lonely and sorrowful, in his stately home.

In that noble palace, long ranges of galleries and chambers were filled with objects of art and taste, beautiful and costly and refined. If a yard of the wall had looked bare, it would have been adorned forthwith by some trophy of barbaric arms taken in warfare. If a corner had seemed empty, it would have been at once filled with an exquisite group of marble, wrought into still life by some Greek artist's chisel. Not a recess in that pile of building, but spoke of comfort, complete in every respect, and the only empty chamber in the whole, was its owner's heart. Nay, more than empty, for it was haunted by the ghost of a beloved memory, and the happiness that was never to come again.

Cold and dreary is the air of that mysterious tenement where we buried our treasures long ago. Cold and dreary like the atmosphere of the tomb, but a perfume hangs about it still, because love, being divine, is therefore eternal; and though the turf be laid damp and heavy over the beloved head, our tears fall like the blessed rain from heaven, and water the very barrenness of the grave, till at length, through weary patience and humble resignation, the flowers of hope begin to spring, and faith tells us they shall bloom hereafter, in another and a better world.

Licinius was very lonely, and at a time of life when, perhaps, loneliness is most oppressive to the mind. Youth has so much to anticipate, is so full of hope, is so sanguine, so daring, that its own dreams are sufficient for its sustenance; but in middle age, men have already found out that the mirage is but sand and sunshine after all; they look forward, indeed, still, yet only from habit, and because the excitement that was once such intoxicating rapture, is now but a necessary stimulant. If they have no ties of family, no affections to take them out of themselves, they become pompous triflers, or despondent recluses, according as their temperaments lead them to inordinate self-importance or excessive humility. Not so when the quiver is full, and the hearth is merry with the patter of little feet, and the ring of childish laughter. There is a charm to dispel all the evil, and call up all the good, even of the worst man's nature, in the soft, white brow, pure from the stamp of sin and care, in the bold, bright eyes that look up so trustingly to his own. There is a sense of protection and responsibility, that few natures are so depraved as to repudiate, in the household relationship which acknowledges and obeys the father as its head; and there is no man so callous or so reckless, but he would wish to appear nobler and better than he is, in the eyes of his child.

Licinius had none of these incentives to virtue, but the lofty nature and the loving heart that could worship a memory, and feel that it was a reality still, had kept him pure from vice. He had never of late attached himself much to anything, till Esca became an inmate of his household; but since he had been in habits of daily intercourse with the Briton, a feeling of content, and well-being, he would have found it difficult to analyse, had gradually crept over him. Perhaps he would have remained unconscious of his slave's influence, had it not been for the blank occasioned by his departure. He missed him sadly now, and wondered why, at every moment of the day, he found himself thinking of the pleasant, familiar face, and frank, cordial smile.

So much alone, he had acquired grave habits of reflection, even of that self-examination which is so beneficial an exercise when impartially performed, but which men so rarely practise without a self-deception that obviates all its good effects. This evening he was in a more thoughtful mood than common; this evening, more than ever, it seemed to him that his was an aimless, fruitless life; that he had let the material pleasures of existence slip through his fingers, and taken nothing in exchange. Of what availed his toils, his enterprise, his love of country, his self-denial, his endurance of hardship and privation? What was he the better now, that he had marched, and watched, and bled, and preserved whole colonies for the empire, and sat glorious, crowned with laurels in the triumphal car? He looked round on his stately walls, and the trophies that adorned them, thinking the while that even such a home as this might be purchased too dear at the expense of a life-time. Gold and marble, corridors and columns, ivory couches and Tyrian carpets, were these equivalents for youth's toil and manhood's care, and at last a desolate old age? What was this ambition that led men so irresistibly up the steepest paths, by the brink of such fatal precipices? Had he ever experienced its temptations? He scarcely knew. He could not realize them now. Had Guenebra lived, indeed, and had she been his own, he might have prized honour and renown, and a name that was on all men's lips, for her dear sake. To see the kind eyes brighten, to call up a smile into the beloved face, that would surely have been reward enough, and that would never be. Then he fell to thinking of the bright days when they were all-in-all to each other, when the very sky seemed fairer, while he watched for her white dress under the oak-tree. Was he not perfectly happy then? Would he not at least have been perfectly happy, could he have called her, as he hoped to do, his own? Honesty answered, No. At the very best there was a vague longing, a something wanting, a sense of insufficiency, of insecurity, and even discontent. If it was so then, how had it been since? Passing over the sharp, sudden stroke so numbing his senses at the time, that a long interval had to elapse ere he awoke to its full agony—passing over the subsequent days of yearning, and nights of vain regret, the desolation that laid waste a heart which would bear fruit no more, he reviewed the long years in which he had striven to make duty and the love of country fill the void, and was forced to confess that here, too, all was barren. There was a something ever wanting, even to complete the dull torpor of that resignation which philosophy inculcated, and common-sense enjoined. What was it? Licinius could not answer his own question, though he felt that it must have some solution, at which man's destiny intended him to arrive.

All the Roman knew, all he could realize, was,

that the spring was gone long ago, with her buds of promise, and her laughing morning skies; that the glory of summer had passed away, with its lustrous beauty and its burnished plains, and its deep, dark foliage quivering in the heat; that the blast of autumn had strewn the cold earth now with faded flowers and withered leaves, and all the wreck of all the hopes that blossomed so tenderly, and bloomed so bright and fair. The heaven was cold and grey, and between him and heaven the bare branches waved and nodded mocking, pointing with spectral fingers to the dull, cheerless sky. Could he but have believed, could he but have vaguely imaged to himself that there would come another spring, that belief, that vague imagining had been to Licinius, the one inestimable treasure for which he would have bartered all else in the world.

In vain he sought, and looked about him for something on which to lean, for something out of, and superior to himself, inspiring him with that sense of being protected, for which humanity feels so keen, yet so indefinite a desire. What is the bravest and wisest of mankind, but a child in the dark, groping for the parental hand that shall guide its uncertain steps? Where was he to find the ideal that he could honestly worship, on the superiority of which he could heartily depend? The mythology of Rome, degraded as it had become, was not yet stripped of all the graceful attributes it owed to its Hellenic origin. That which was Greek, might indeed be evil, yet it could scarce fail to be fair; but what rational man could ground his faith on the theocracy of Olympus, or contemplate with any feeling save disgust, that material Pantheism, in which the lowest even of human vices was exalted into a divinity? As well become a worshipper of Isis at once, and prostitute, to the utter degradation of the body, all the noblest and fairest imagery of the mind. No, the deities that Homer sang were fit subjects for the march of those Greek hexameters, sonorous and majestic as the roll of the Ægean sea; fit types of sensuous perfection, to be wrought by the Greek chisel, from out the veined blocks of smooth, white Parian stone; but for man, intellectual man, to bow down before the crafty Hermes, or the thick-witted god of forges, or the ambrosial front of father Jove himself, the least ideal of all, was a simple absurdity, that could scarce impose upon a woman or a child.

Licinius had served in the East, and he bethought him now of a nation against whom he had stood in arms, brave, fierce soldiers, men instinct with public virtue and patriotism, whose rites, different from those of all other races, were observed with scrupulous fidelity and self-denial. This people, he had heard, worshipped a God of whom there was no material type, whose being was omnipresent and spiritual, on whom they implicitly depended when all else failed, and trusting in whom they never feared to die. But they admitted none to partake with them in their advantages, and their faith seemed to inculcate hatred of the stranger, no less than dissensions and strife amongst themselves.

"Is there nothing, alas! but duty, stern, cold duty to fill this void?" thought Licinius. "Be it so, then, my sword shall be once more at the service of my country, and I will die in my harness like a Roman and a soldier at the last!"

CHAPTER VII.

"HABET!"

HIPPIAS, the fencing-master, had completed his preparations for the night. With a certain military instinct, as necessary to his profession as to that of the legitimate soldier, he could rely upon his own dispositions, when they were once made, with perfect confidence, and a total absence of anxiety for the result.

Like all men habituated to constant strife, he was never so completely in his element as when surrounded by perils, only to be warded off by cool, vigilant courage; and though he may have had moments in which he longed for the softer joys of affection and repose, it needed but the clang of a buckler or the gleam of a sword to rouse him into his fiercer self once more.

It had been his habit to attend Valeria, for the purpose of instructing her in swordmanship, by an hour's practice on certain appointed days. Everything connected with the amphitheatre possessed at this period such a morbid fascination for all classes of the Roman people, that even ladies of rank esteemed it a desirable accomplishment to understand the use of the sword; and it is said that on more than one occasion women of noble birth had been known to take part in the deadly games themselves. These, however, were rare instances of such complete defiance of all modesty and even natural feeling; but to thrust, and shout, and stamp in the conflict of mimic warfare was simply esteemed the regular exercise and the healthy excitement of every patrician dame who aspired to a fashionable reputation. Such sudorifics, accompanied by excessive use of the bath and a free indulgence in slaking the thirst, arising from so severe a course of treatment, must have been highly detrimental to female beauty; but even this consideration was postponed to the absorbing claims of fashion, and then, as now, a woman was content and pleased to disfigure herself by any process, however painful and inconvenient, providing other women did the same.

It is possible, too, that the manly symmetry of form, the tough thews and sinews of their instructors were not without effect on pupils, whose hearts softened in proportion as their muscles became hard, and whose whole habits and education tended to interest them in the person and profession of the gladiator. Be this as it may, the fencing-masters of Rome had but little time left on their hands, and, of these, Hippias was doubtless the most sought after by the fair.

It was his custom to neglect nothing, however trifling, connected with his calling. No details were too small to be attended to by one whose daily profession taught him that life and victory might depend on the mere quiver of an eyelid, the accidental slip of a buckle; and, besides, he took a strange pride in his deadly trade, and especially in the methodical regularity with which he carried it out.

Though bound to-night for the desperate enterprise which should make or mar him; though confident that, in either event, he would to-morrow be far beyond the necessities of a gladiator, it was part of his character to play out his part thoroughly to-day. Valeria would expect him, as usual, before the bathing-hour on the following morning. It was but decent he should leave a message at her house that he might be detained. The very wording of his excuse brought to his mind the possibilities of the next few hours—the many chances of failure in the enterprise, failure which, to him at least, the leader of desperate men, was synonymous with certain death. To-day, for the first time, as he turned his steps towards her mansion, a soft, half-sorrowful, yet not unpleasing sensation stole into his heart as the image of its mistress rose before him in all the pride of her stately beauty.

He had often admired the regularity of her haughty features—had scanned, in his own critical way, with unqualified approval the lines of her noble figure, and the symmetry of her firm, well-turned limbs; had even longed to touch that wealth of silken hair when it shook loose in her exertions, and yet—a strange sensation for such a man—had flinched and felt oppressed when, placing her once in a position of defence, a tress of it had fallen across his hand. Now, it seemed to him that he would give much to live those few moments over again; that he would like to see her once more, if, indeed, as was probable, it would be for the last time; that there was no other woman to be compared with her in Rome; and that, with all her glowing beauty and all her physical attractions, her pride was her greatest charm.

He was a desperate man, about to play a desperate game for life. Such thoughts in such a heart and at such a time quicken with fearful rapidity into evil. Admiration, untempered by the holier leavening of that affection which can only exist in the breast that has kept itself pure, soon grows to cruelty and selfishness. The love of beauty, poisoned by the love of strife, seethes into a fierce passionate longing, less that of the lover for his mistress than of the tiger for its prey. Valeria was a proud woman, the proudest and the fairest in Rome. He drew his breath hard as he thought what a wild triumph it would be to bend that stately neck, and humble that pride to his very feet.

Methodical and soldier-like, he had seen to everything with his own eyes. The plot was laid, the conspirators were armed and instructed, there was yet an hour or two to spare before the appointed gathering at the Tribune's house, and that time he resolved should be devoted to Valeria; at least, he would feast his eyes once more on that glorious beauty, of which he now seemed to acknowledge the full power. He would see her, would bid her farewell. She had always welcomed him cordially and kindly; perhaps she would be sorry to lose him altogether. He smiled a very evil smile, though his heart beat faster than it had done since he was a boy, as he halted under the statue of Hermes in her porch.

And Valeria was sitting in her chamber, with her head buried in her hands, and her long brown hair sweeping like a mantle to her feet. All the feelings that could most goad and madden a woman were tearing at her heart. She dared not—for the sake of tottering reason she *dared* not—think of the Tribune's white face and dropping jaw, and limbs strewed helpless on the couch. She suffered the vision, indeed, to weigh upon her like some oppressive nightmare; but she abstained, with an effort of which she was yet fully conscious, from analysing its meaning or recalling its details, above all, from considering its origin and its effect. No! the image of Esca still filled her brain and her heart. Esca in the amphitheatre; Esca chained, and sleeping on the hard, hot pavement; Esca walking by her side through the shady streets; and Esca turning away with his noble figure and his manly step, exulting in the liberty that set him free from *her!*

Then came a rush of those softer feelings, that were required to render her torture unbearable: the sting of "what might have been;" the picture of herself (she could see herself in her mind's eye —beautiful and fascinating, in all the advantages of dress and jewels) leaning on that strong arm, and the kind, brave face looking down into hers with the protective air that became it so well. To give him all; to tell him all she had risked, all she had done for his sake, and to hear his loving accents in reply! She almost fancied in her dream that this had actually come to pass, so vividly did her heart image to itself its dearest longings. Then she saw another figure in the place that ought to be her own—another face into which he was looking as he had never looked in hers. It was the dark eyed girl's! The dark-eyed girl, who had been her rival throughout! Would *she* have done as much for him with her pale face and her frightened, shrinking ways? And now, ere this, he had reached her home, was whispering in her ear, with his arm round her waist. Perhaps he was boasting of the conquest he had made over the haughty Roman lady, and telling her that he had scorned Valeria for her dear sake. Then all that was evil in her nature gained the ascendant, and with the bitter recklessness that has ruined so many an undisciplined heart, she said to herself—"There is no reality but evil. Life is an illusion, and hope a lie. It matters little what becomes of me now!"

When Myrrhina entered she found her lady busied in rearranging the folds of her robe and her disordered tresses. It was no part of Valeria's character to show by her outward bearing what was passing in her mind, and least of all would she have permitted her attendant to guess at the humiliation she had undergone. The waiting-maid, indeed, was a little puzzled; but she had gained so much knowledge, both by observation and experience, of the strange effects produced by over-excitement on her sex, that she never suffered herself to be surprised at a feminine vagary of any description. Now, though she wondered why Esca was gone, and why her mistress was so reserved and haughty, she refrained discreetly from question or remark, contenting herself with a silent offer of her services, and arranging the brown hair into a plaited coronet on Valeria's brows, without betraying by her manner that she was conscious anything unusual had taken place.

After a few moments' silence, her mistress's voice was sufficiently steadied for her to speak.

"I did not send for you," said she. "What do you want here?"

Myrrhina's hands were busied with the long silken tresses, and she held a comb between her teeth. Nevertheless, she answered volubly.

"I would not have disturbed you, madam, this warm, sultry evening—and I rebuked the porter soundly for letting him in; only as he said, to be sure, he never was denied before, and I thought, perhaps, you would not be displeased to see him, if it was only for a few minutes, and he seemed so anxious and hurried—and, indeed, he never has much time to spare, so I bade him wait in the inner hall while I came to let you know."

Hoping even against hope! She knew it was impossible, yet her heart leapt as she thought—"Oh! if it were only Esca who had turned back!"

"I will see him," said she, quietly, prolonging the illusion by purposely avoiding to ask who this untimely visitor might be.

In another minute Hippias stood before her—Hippias, the fencing-master, a man in whose dangerous career she had always taken a vague interest; whose personal prowess she admired, and whose reputation, such as it was, possessed for her a wild fascination of its own. He was reckless, too, from the very nature of his profession; and she, in her present mood, more reckless, more desperate than any gladiator of them all. It would have done her good to stand, with naked steel, against some fierce wild beast or deadly foe. There was nothing, she felt, that she could not dare to-day. Nerve and brain wound up to the highest pitch of excitement—heart and feelings crushed, and wounded, and sore. When the reaction came, it would necessarily be fatal; when the tide ebbed, it would leave a wearied, helpless sufferer on the shore.

Such was the frame of mind in which Valeria received the gladiator; outwardly impassive—for her colour did not even deepen, nor her breath come quicker at his unexpected appearance—inwardly vexed by a conflict of tumultuous feelings, and longing for any change—any anodyne that could deaden or alleviate her pain. How could she but respond to his manly, respectful "farewell?" How could she but listen to the few burning words in which he spoke of long-suppressed and hopeless adoration, or pretend not to be interested in the desperate enterprise which he hinted might prevent his ever looking on her fair face again. He soothed her self-love; he roused her curiosity; he set her pride on its broken pedestal again, and propped it with a strong, yet gentle hand; and so the two thunder-clouds drew nearer still and nearer, ere they met, to be destroyed and riven by the lightning their own contact had engendered.

CHAPTER VIII.

TOO LATE!

ESCA, treading on air, hastened from Valeria's house with the common selfishness of love, ignoring all the pain and disappointment he had left behind him. The young blood coursed merrily through his veins, and in spite of his anxiety, he exulted in the sense of being at liberty once more. He was alive, doubtless, to the generosity and devotion of the woman who had set him free, nor was he so blind as to be unaware of the affection that had driven her to such desperate measures for his sake; and in the first glow of a gratitude, that had in it no vestige of tenderer feelings, he had resolved, when his mission was accomplished and Mariamne placed in safety, he would return and throw himself at the Roman lady's feet once more. But the further he left her stately porch behind, the weaker became this generous resolution, and ere long he had little difficulty in persuading himself that his first duty was to the Jewess, and that in his future actions he must be guided by circumstances, or, in other words, follow the bent of his own inclinations. Meanwhile, in spite of his wounded foot, he sped on towards the Tiber as fast as, in years gone by, he had followed the lean wolf, or the foam-flecked boar, over the green hills of Britain.

The sun had not been down an hour when he entered the well-known street that was now enchanted ground; yet, while he looked up into the darkening sky, his heart turned sick within him at the thought that he might be too late, after all.

The garden-door was open, as she must have left it. She was not, therefore, in the house. He might find her at the river-side, and have the happiness of a few minutes alone with her, ere he brought her back and placed her, for the second time, in safety within her father's walls. The more prudent course, he confessed to himself at the time, would have been to alarm Eleazar, and put him on the defensive at once; but he had been so long without seeing Mariamne, the peril in which she was placed had so endeared her to him, and his own near approach to death had stamped her image so vividly on his heart, that he could not resist the temptation of seeking her at the water-side, and telling her, unwatched by other ears or eyes, all he had felt and endured since they last parted, and how, for both their sakes, they must never part again.

Full of such thoughts, he ran down to the water's edge, and sought the broken column where she was accustomed to descend and fill her pitcher from the stream. In vain his eager eye watched for the dark-clad figure and the dear pale face. Once in the deepening twilight his heart leapt as he thought he saw her crouching low beneath the bank, and sank again to find he had been deceived by a fallen slab of stone. Then he turned for one more searching look ere he departed, and his glance rested on a pitcher, broken into a dozen fragments, at his feet.

He did not know that it was Mariamne's. How should he, when a thousand pitchers carried by a thousand women to the Tiber every evening were precisely alike? Yet his blood ran cold through his veins and his fears hurried him back, almost insensibly, to Eleazar's door, which he burst open without going through the ceremony of knocking.

Her father and his brother were in the house. The former leapt to his feet and snatched a javelin from the wall ere he recognized his visitor. The latter, less prone to do battle at a moment's notice, laid his hand on Eleazar's arm, and calmly said—

"It is the friend who is always welcome, and whom we have expected day by day in vain."

Everything looked so much as usual that for a moment Esca felt almost reassured. It was possible Mariamne might be even now busied with household affairs, safe in the inner chamber. A lover's bashfulness brought the blood to his cheeks, as he reflected if it were so, it would be difficult to account for his unceremonious entrance; but the recollection of her danger soon stifled all such trivial considerations, and he confronted her father impetuously, and asked him, almost in a threatening tone,

"Where is Mariamne?"

Eleazar looked first simply astonished, then somewhat offended. He answered, however, with more command of temper than was his wont.

"My daughter has but now left the house with her pitcher. She will be home again almost immediately, but what is this to thee?"

"What is it to me?" repeated Esca in a voice of thunder, catching hold of his questioner's arm at the same time with an iron grasp for which the fierce old Jew liked him none the worse—"What is it to thee, to him, to all of us? I tell thee, old man, whilst we are drivelling here, they are bearing her off into captivity ten thousand times worse than death! I heard the plot—I heard it with my own ears, lying chained like a dog on the hard stones. The wicked Tribune was to make her his own this very night, and though he has met his reward, the villains that do his bidding have got her in their power ere this. The pure,—the loved—the beautiful—Mariamne—Mariamne!"

He hid his face in his hands, and his strong frame shook with agony from head to heel.

It was the turn of Calchas now to start to his feet, and look about him as if in search of a weapon. His first impulse was resistance to oppression, even by the strong hand.

With Eleazar, on the contrary, the instincts of the soldier predominated, and the very magnitude of the emergency seemed to endow him with preternatural coolness and composure.

He knit his thick brows indeed, and there was a smothered glare in his eye that boded no good to an enemy when the time for an outbreak should arrive, but his voice was low and distinct, as in a few sharp eager questions he gathered the outline of the plot that was to rob him of his daughter. Then he thought for a few seconds ere he spoke.

"The men that were to take her? What were they like? I would fain know them if I came across them."

His white teeth gleamed like a wild beast's with a smile ominous of his intentions on their behalf.

"Damasippus and Oarses," replied the Briton. "The former stout, sleek, heavy, and beetle-browed. The latter pale, dark, and thin. An Egyptian with an Egyptian's false face, and more than an Egyptian's cruelty and cunning."

"Where live they?" asked the Jew, buckling at the same time a formidable two-edged sword to his side.

"In the Flaminian Way," replied the other. "High up in some garret where we should never find them. But they will not take her there. She is by this time at the other end of the city in the Tribune's house." And again he groaned in anguish of spirit at the thought.

"And that house?" asked Eleazar, still busied with his warlike preparations. "How is it defended? I know its outside well, and an easy entrance from the wall to the inner court; but what resistance shall we encounter within? what force can the Tribune's people raise at a moment's outcry?"

"Alas!" answered Esca. "To-night of all nights, the house of Placidus is garrisoned like a fortress. A chosen band of gladiators are to sup with the Tribune, and afterwards to take possession of the palace and drag Cæsar from the throne. When they find the banquet prepared for them, I know them too well to think they will separate without partaking of it, even though their host be lying dead on the festal couch. She will become the prey of men like Hippias, Lutorius, and Euchenor. But if we cannot rescue her, at least we may die in the attempt."

Even in his anxiety for his daughter such news as this could not but startle the emissary of the Jewish nation. In an instant's time he had run over its importance, as it regarded his own mission and the probable influence on the destinies of his country. Should the conspiracy succeed Vitellius might already be numbered with the dead, and instead of that easy self-indulgent glutton, over whom he had already obtained considerable influence, he would have to do with the bold, sagacious, far-seeing general, the remorseless enemy of his nation, whom neither he nor any of his countrymen had ever succeeded in deceiving by stratagem or worsting by force of arms. When the purple descended on Vespasian the doom of Jerusalem was sealed. Nevertheless, Eleazar concentrated his mind on the present emergency. In a few words he laid out his plan for the rescue of his daughter.

"The freedmen's garret must be our first point of attack," said he. "The Tribune would scarce have ordered them to bring their prize to his house to-night, where there would be so many to dispute it with him, and where dissension would be fatal to his great enterprise. Calchas and I will proceed immediately to the dwelling of this Damasippus and his fellow-villain. Your directions will enable us to find it. You, Esca, speed off at once to the Tribune's house. You will soon learn whether she has been brought there. If so come to us without delay in the Flaminian Way. I am not entirely without friends even here, and I will call on two or three of my people to help as I go along. Young man, you are bold and true. We will have her out of the Tribune's house if we pull the walls down with our naked hands; and let me but come within reach of the villains who take shelter there"—here his face darkened and his frame quivered in a paroxysm of suppressed fury—"may my father's tomb be dishonoured, and the name of my mother defiled, if I dip not my hands to the very elbows in their hearts' blood!"

To be told he was brave and true by her father added fuel to Esca's enthusiasm. It was indeed much for Eleazar to confess on behalf of a stranger and a heathen, but the fierce old warrior's heart warmed to a kindred nature that seemed incapable of selfish fear, and he approved hugely, moreover, of the implicit attention with which the Briton listened to his directions, and his readiness for instantaneous action however desperate.

Calchas, too, clasped the young man warmly by the hand. "We are but three," said he, "three against a host. Yet I have no fear. I trust in

One who never failed his servants yet. One to whom emperors and legions are as a handful of dust before the wind, or a few dried thorns on the beacon-fire. And so do you, my son, so do you, though you know it not. But the time shall come when His very benefits shall compel you to confess your Master, and when in sheer gratitude you shall enrol yourself amongst those who serve Him faithfully even unto death."

Many a time during that eventful and anxious night had Esca occasion to remember the old man's solemn words. Its horrors, its catastrophes, its alternations of hope and fear, might have driven one mad, who had nothing to depend upon but his own unaided strength and resolution. Few great actions have been performed, few tasks exacting the noble heroism of endurance fulfilled successfully, without extraneous aid, without the help of some leading principle out of, and superior to, the man. Honour, patriotism, love, loyalty, all have supported their votaries through superhuman exertions and difficulties that seemed insurmountable, teaching them to despise dangers and hardships with a courage sterner than mortals are expected to possess; but none of these can impart that confidence which is born of faith in the believer's breast;—that confidence which enables him to take good and evil with an equal mind, to look back on the past without a sigh, forward on the future without a fear; and though the present may be all a turmoil of peril, uncertainty, and confusion, to stand calmly in the midst, doing the best he can with a stout heart and an unruffled brow, while he leaves the result fearlessly and trustfully in the hand of God.

Eleazar and Calchas were already equipped for the pursuit. The one armed to the teeth, and looking indeed a formidable enemy; the other mild and hopeful as usual, venerable with his white hair and beard, and carrying but a simple staff for his weapon.

In grave silence, but with a grasp of the hand more emphatic than any spoken words, the three parted on their search. Esca threading his way at once through the narrow and devious streets that led towards the Tribune's house,—that house which he had left so gladly but a few short hours ago when, rescued by Valeria, he bade her farewell, exulting in the liberty that enabled him to seek Mariamne's side once more.

He soon reached the hated dwelling. All there seemed quiet as the grave. From other quarters of the city indeed there came, now and again, the roar of distant voices which rose and fell at intervals as the tide of tumult ebbed and flowed, but, preoccupied as he was, Esca took little heed of these ominous sounds, for they bore him no intelligence of Mariamne. All was silent in the porch, all was silent in the vestibule and outer hall, but as he ventured across its marble pavement, he heard the bustle of preparation, and the din of flagons within.

It was at the risk of liberty and life, that he crept noiselessly forward, and peeped into the banqueting-hall, which was already partially lighted up for the feast. Shrinking behind a column, he observed the slaves, many of whom he knew well by sight, laying covers, burnishing vases, and otherwise making ready for a sumptuous entertainment. He listened for a few moments, hoping to gather from their conversation some news of the Jewess and her captors.

All at once he started and trembled violently. Bold as he was, in common with his northern countrymen a vein of superstition ran through his nature, and though he feared nothing tangible or corporeal, he held in considerable dread all that touched upon the confines of the spiritual and the unknown. There within ten paces of him, ghastly pale, with dark circles round his eyes, and clad in white, stood the figure of the Tribune, pointing, as it seemed to him, with shadowy hand at the different couches, and giving directions in a low sepulchral voice for the order of the banquet.

"Not yet!" he heard the apparition exclaim in tones of languid, fretful impatience. "Not come yet! the idle loiterers! Well, she must preside there at the supper-table and take her place at once as mistress here. Ho! slaves! bring more flowers! Fill the tall golden cup with Falernian and set it next to mine!"

Well did Esca know to whom these directions must refer. Though his blood had been chilled for an instant by this reappearance, as he believed it, of his enemy from the grave, he soon collected his scattered energies and summoned his courage back, with the hateful conviction that, alive or dead, the Tribune was resolved to possess himself of Mariamne. And this he vowed to prevent, ay, though he should slay his dark-eyed love with his own hand.

It was obvious now that Damasippus and Oarses would bring the captive straight to their patron's house, that Eleazar and Calchas had gone upon a fool's errand to the freedmen's garret in the Flaminian Way. What would he have given to be cheered by the wise counsels of the one, and backed by the strong arm of the other! Would there be time for him to slip from here unobserved, and to summon them to his aid? Three desperate men might cut their way through all the slaves that Placidus could muster, and if they had any chance of success at all it must be before the arrival of the gladiators. But then she was obviously expected every minute. She might arrive—horrible thought!—while he was gone for help, and once in the Tribune's power it would be too late.

In his despair the words of Calchas recurred forcibly to his mind. "We are but three," said the old man, "three against a host, yet I have no fear." And Esca resolved that though he was but one, he too would have no fear, but would trust implicitly in the award of eternal justice, which would surely interfere to prevent this unholy sacrifice.

Feeling that his sword was loose in its sheath and ready to his hand, holding his breath, and nerving himself for the desperate effort he might be called upon at any moment to make, the

Briton stole softly back through the vestibule, and concealed himself behind a marble group in the darkest corner of the porch. Here, with the dogged courage of his race, he made up his mind that he would await the arrival of Mariamne, and rescue her at all hazards, against any odds, or die with her in the attempt.

CHAPTER IX.

THE LURE.

LIKE other great cities, the poorer quarters of Rome were densely crowded. The patricians, and indeed all the wealthier class, affected rural tastes even in the midst of the capital, and much space was devoted to the gardens and pleasure-grounds which surrounded their dwellings. The humbler inhabitants were consequently driven to herd together in great numbers with little regard to health or convenience, and the streets leading to and adjoining the Tiber were perhaps the most thickly populated of all. That in which Eleazar's house stood, was seldom empty of passengers at any hour of the twenty-four, and least of all about sunset when the women thronged out of their dwellings to draw water for the household consumption of the following day.

Oarses was well aware of this, and therefore it was that the cunning Egyptian had protested against an abduction of the Jewish maiden by open force from her father's door. "Leave it to me," said this finished villain, in discussing their infamous project with his patron. "I know a lure to wile such birds as these off the bough into my open hand. Stratagem first, force afterwards. There is no need to waken the tongues of all the women in the quarter. It was the cackling of a goose, my patron, that foiled the attack on the Capitol."

Mariamne, anxious and sad, was carrying her pitcher listlessly down to the Tiber and letting her thoughts wander far from her occupation, into a few sweet memories, and a thousand dreary apprehensions, when she was accosted by a dark sallow old woman, whose speech and manners, as well as her dress, betrayed an Eastern origin. The stranger asked some trifling questions about her way, and prayed for a draught of cold water when the pitcher should be filled, and Mariamne, whose heart unconsciously warmed to the homely Syriac, entered freely into conversation with one of her own sex, and whose language denoted, moreover, that she was familiar with her nation.

Willingly she drew her a measure from the stream, which the other quaffed with the moderation of one whose thirst is habitually quenched with wine rather than water.

"It is somewhat muddy, I fear," said the girl, kindly reverting in her own mind to the sparkling fountains of her native land, and yet acknowledging how she loved this turbid stream better than them all. "If you will come back with me to my father's house I can offer you a draught of wine and a morsel of bread to cheer you on your way."

The other, though with no great avidity, took a second pull at the pitcher.

"Nay," said she, "my daughter, I will not tax your hospitality so far. Nor have I need. There is lore enough left under these faded locks of mine, to turn the foulest cesspool in Rome as clear as crystal. Ay, to change this tasteless draught to wine of Lebanon, and the pitcher that contains it to a vase of gold."

Mariamne shrank from her with a gesture of dismay. Believing implicitly in their power, her religion forbade her to hold any intercourse with those who professed the black art.

The other marked her repugnance. "My

child," she continued in soothing tones, "be not afraid of the old woman's secret gifts. Mine is but a harmless knowledge, gained by study of the ancient Chaldæan scrolls, such as your own wise king possessed of old. It is but white magic, such as your high-priest himself would not scruple to employ. Fear not, I say—I, who have pored over those mystic characters till mine eyes grew dim, can read your sweet pale face as plain as the brazen tablets in the Forum, and I can see in it sorrow, and care, and anxiety for him you love."

Mariamne started. It was true enough, but how could the wise woman have found it out? The girl looked wistfully at her companion, and the latter, satisfied she was on the right track, proceeded to answer that questioning glance. "Yes," she said, "you think he is in danger or in grief. You wonder why you do not see him oftener. Sometimes you fear he may be false. What would you not give, my poor child, to look on the golden locks, and the white brow, now, at this very moment? And I can show them to you if you will. The old woman is not ungrateful even for a draught of the Tiber's muddy stream."

The blood mounted to Mariamne's brow, but

the light kindled at the same time in her eyes, and the soft gleam swept over her face, that comes into every human countenance when the heart vibrates with an allusion to its treasure as though the silver cord thrilled to the touch of an angel's wing. It was no clumsy guess of the wise woman, to infer that this dark-eyed damsel cherished some fair-haired lover.

"What mean you?" asked the girl, eagerly. "How can you show him to me? What do you know of him? Is he safe? Is he happy?"

The wise woman smiled. Here was a bird flying blindfold into the net. Take her by her affections, and there would be little difficulty in the capture.

"He is in danger," she replied. "But you could save him if you only knew how. He might be happy too, if he would. But with another!'

To do Mariamne justice she heard only the first sentence.

"In danger!" she repeated, "and I could save him! Oh, tell me where he is, and what I can do for his sake!"

The wise woman pulled a small mirror from her bosom. "I cannot tell you," she answered, "but I can show him to you in this. Only not here, where the shadow of a passer-by might destroy the charm. Let us turn aside to that vacant space by the broken column, and you shall look without interruption on the face you love."

It was but a short way off, though the ruins which surrounded it made the place lonely and secluded; had it been twice the distance, however, Mariamne would have accompanied her new acquaintance without hesitation in her eagerness for tidings of Esca's fate. As she neared the broken column, so endeared to her by associations, she could not repress a faint sigh which was not lost on her companion.

"It was here you met him before," whispered the wise woman. "It is here you shall see his face again."

This was scarcely a random shaft, for it required little penetration to discover that Mariamne had some tender associations connected with a spot thus adapted for the meeting of a pair of lovers; nevertheless the apparent familiarity with her previous actions, was sufficient to convince the Jewess of her companion's supernatural knowledge, and though it roused alarm, it excited curiosity in a still greater degree.

"Take the mirror in your hand," whispered the

wise woman, when they had reached the column, casting, at the same time, a searching glance around. "Shut your eyes whilst I speak the charm that calls him, three times over, and then look steadily on its surface till I have counted a hundred."

Mariamne obeyed these directions implicitly. Standing in the vacant space with the mirror in her hand, she shut her eyes and listened intently to the solemn tones of the wise woman chanting in a low monotonous voice some unintelligible stanzas, while from the deep shadow behind the broken column, there stole out the portly figure of Damasippus, and, at the same moment, half a dozen strong well-armed slaves rose from the different hiding-places in which they lay concealed amongst the ruins.

Ere the incantation had been twice repeated, Damasippus threw a shawl over the girl's head, muffling her so completely, while he caught her in his strong arms, that an outcry was impossible. The others snatched her up ere she could make a movement, and bore her swiftly off to a chariot with four white horses waiting in the next street, whilst the wise woman following at a rapid pace, and disencumbering herself of her female attire as she sped along, disclosed the cunning features and the thin wiry form of Oarses the Egyptian.

Coming up with Damasippus, who was panting behind the slaves and their burden, he laughed a low noiseless laugh.

"My plan was the best," said he, "after all. What fools these women are, oh my friend! Is there any other creature that can be taken with a bait so simple? Three inches of mirror, and the ghost of an absent face!"

But Damasippus had not breath to reply. Hurrying onward he was chiefly anxious to dispose of his prize in the chariot without interruption; and when he reached it he mounted by her side, and bidding Oarses and the slaves follow as near as was practicable, he drove off at great speed in the direction of the Tribune's house.

But this was an eventful night in Rome, and although for that reason well adapted to a deed of violence, its tumult and confusion exacted great caution from those who wished to proceed without interruption along the streets.

The shouts that had disturbed the two freedmen in their garret whilst preparing the enterprise they had since so successfully carried out, gave no false warning of the coming storm. That storm had burst, and was now raging in its fury throughout a wide portion of the city. Like all such outbreaks it gathered force and violence in many quarters at once, and from many sources unconnected with its original cause.

Rome was the theatre that night of a furious civil war, consequent on the intrigues of various parties which had now grown to a head.

The old Prætorian Guard had been broken up by Vitellius, and dismissed without any of the honours and gratuities to which they considered themselves entitled, in order to make way for another body of troops on whose fidelity the Emperor believed he could rely, and who were now called, in contradistinction to their predecessors, the New Prætorians. Two such conflicting interests carried in them the elements of the direst hatred and strife. The original bodyguard hoping to be restored by Vespasian, should he attain the purple, had everything to gain by a change of dynasty, and were easily won over by the partisans of that successful general to any enterprise, however desperate, which would place him on the throne. Trusting to this powerful aid, these partisans, of whom Julius Placidus, the Tribune, though he had wormed himself into the confidence of Vitellius, was one of the most active and unscrupulous, were ready enough to raise the standard of revolt and had no fear for the result. The train was laid, and to-night it had been decided that the match should be applied. In regular order of battle, in three ranks with spears advanced and eagles in the centre, the Old Prætorians marched at sundown to attack the camp of their successors. It was a bloody and obstinate contest. The new body-guard, proud of their promotion, and loyal to the hand that had bought them, defended themselves to the death. Again and again was the camp almost carried. Again and again were the assailants obstinately repulsed. It was only when slain, man by man, falling in their ranks as they stood, with all their wounds *in front,* that a victory was obtained—a victory which so crippled the conquerors as to render them but inefficient auxiliaries in the other conflicts of that eventful night. But this was only one of the many pitched battles, so to speak, of which Rome was the unhappy theatre. The Capitol after an obstinate defence had been taken by the partisans of the present Emperor and burned to the ground.

This stronghold having been previously seized

and occupied by Sabinus, who declared himself Governor of Rome in the name of Vespasian, and who even received in state several of the principal nobility and a deputation from the harassed and vacillating senate, had been alternately the object of attack and defence to either party. Its possession seemed to confer a spurious sovereignty over the whole city, and it was held as obstinately as it was vigorously and desperately attacked.

An hour or two before sunset, an undisciplined body of soldiers, armed only with their swords, and formidable chiefly from the wild fury with which they seemed inspired, marched through the Forum and ascended the Capitoline Hill.

The assailants having no engines of war either for protection or offence, suffered severely from the missiles showered upon them by the besieged, till the thought struck them of throwing flaming torches into the place from the roofs of the houses which surrounded it, and which, erected in time of peace, had been suffered to overtop the Roman citadel. In vain, after the flames had consumed the gate, did they endeavour to force an entrance, for Sabinus, with the unscrupulous resource of a Roman soldier, had blocked the way by a hundred prostrate statues of gods and men, pulled down from the sacred pedestals on which they had stood for ages; but the contiguous houses catching fire, and all the woodwork of the Capitol being old and dry, the flames soon spread, and in a few hours the stronghold of Roman pride and Roman history was levelled with the ground. Callous to the memories around him, forgetful of the Tarquins, and the Scipios, and the many hallowed names that shed their lustre on this monument of his country's greatness, Sabinus lost his presence of mind in proportion as the necessity for preserving it became more urgent. He was no longer able to control his troops, and the latter, panic-stricken with the entrance of their enemies, disbanded, and betook themselves to flight. The majority, including one woman of noble birth, were put ruthlessly to the sword, but a few, resembling their assailants, as they did, in arms, appearance, and language, were fortunate enough to catch the password by which they recognized each other, and so escaped.

In another quarter of the mighty city, a large body of troops who had hoisted the standard of Vespasian, and had already suffered one repulse which rather excited their animosity than quelled their ardour, were advancing in good order, and, according to sound warlike tactics, in three divisions. The gardens of Sallust, laid out by that elegant and intellectual sensualist, with a view to pursuits far removed from strife and bloodshed, were the scene of an obstinate combat, in which however one of these columns succeeded in establishing itself within the walls; and now the struggle that had heretofore been carried on in its outskirts, penetrated to the heart of the Roman capital. The citizens beheld war brought into their very homes and hearths—the familiar street slippery with blood—the wounded soldier reeling on the door-sill, where the children were wont to play—the dead man's limbs strewed helpless by the fountain where the girls assembled with shrill laughing voices on the calm summer evenings,—and worse than all, instead of the kindly grasp of friends and fellow-countrymen, the brother's hand clutching at the brother's throat.

Such horrors, however, did but more demoralize a population already steeped to the very lips in cruelty, vice, and foul iniquity. Trained to bloodshed by the ghastly entertainments of the amphitheatre, the Roman citizen gloated on no spectacle with so keen a pleasure as on the throes of a fellow-creature in the agony of violent death.

The populace seemed now to consider the contest waged at their doors as a goodly show got up for their especial amusement. Loud shouts encouraged the combatants as either party swayed and wavered in the mortal press, and "*Euge!*"—"*Bene!*" were cried as loudly for their encouragement, as if they had been paid gladiators, earning their awful livelihood on the sand. Nay, worse, when some wounded soldier dragged himself into a house for safety, instead of succour, he was received with yells of reprobation, and thrust out into the street that he might be despatched by his conquerors according to the merciless regulations of the amphitheatre.

Nor was man the only demon on the scene. Unsexed women with bare bosoms, wild eyes, streaming hair, and white feet stained with blood, flew to and fro amongst the soldiers, stimulating them to fresh atrocities, with wine and caresses and odious ribald mirth. It was a festival of Death and Sin. She had wreathed her fair arms around the spectral king, and crowned his fleshless brows with her gaudy garlands, and wrapped him in her mantle of flame, and pressed the blood-red goblet to his lips, maddening him with her shrieks of wild, mocking laughter, the while their mutual feet trampled out the lives and souls of their victims on the stones of Rome.

Through a town in such a state of turmoil and confusion, Damasippus took upon himself to conduct in safety the prize he had succeeded in capturing, not, it must be confessed, without many hearty regrets that he had ever embarked in the undertaking.

Devoutly did he now wish that he could shift the whole business on to the shoulders of Oarses; but of late he had been concerned to observe in the patron's manner a certain sense of his own inutility as compared with the astute Egyptian; and if the latter were now permitted to conclude, as he had undoubtedly inaugurated, the adventure, Placidus might be satisfied that there was little use in entertaining two rogues to do the work of one. He knew his patron well enough to be aware of the effect such a conviction would have on his own prospects. The Tribune would no more scruple to bid him go starve or hang, than he would to pull out a superfluous hair from his beard. Therefore, at all risks, thought Damasippus, he must be the man to bring Mariamne into his lord's house.

It was a difficult and a dangerous task. There

was only room for himself and one stout slave besides the charioteer, and the prisoner. The latter had struggled violently, and required to be held down by main force, nor in muffling her screams was it easy to observe the happy medium between silence and suffocation. Also, it was indispensable, in the present lawless state of affairs, to avoid observation; and the spectacle of a handsomely gilded chariot with a female figure in it, held down and closely veiled, the whole drawn by four beautiful white horses, was not calculated to traverse the streets of a crowded city without remark. Oarses, indeed, had suggested a litter, but this had been over-ruled by his comrade on the score of speed, and now the state of the streets made speed impossible. To be sure this enabled the escort to keep up with him, and Damasippus, who was no fighter at heart, derived some comfort from their presence. The darkness, however, which should have favoured him, was dispelled by the numerous conflagrations in various parts of the city; and when the chariot was stopped and forced to turn into a by-street to avoid a crowd rushing towards the blazing Capitol, Damasippus felt his heart sink within him in an access of terror such as even he had never felt before.

CHAPTER X.

FROM SCYLLA TO CHARYBDIS.

UP one street, down another, avoiding the main thoroughfares, now rendered impassable by the tumult, his anxious freedmen threaded their way with difficulty in the direction of the Tribune's house.

Mariamne seemed either to have fainted, or to have resigned herself to her fate, for she had ceased to struggle, and cowered down on the floor of the chariot, silent and motionless. Damasippus trusted his difficulties were nearly over, and resolved never again to be concerned in such an enterprise. Already he imagined himself safe in his patron's porch, claiming the reward of his dexterity, when he was once more arrested by a stoppage which promised a hazardous and protracted delay.

Winding its slow length along, in all the pomp

and dignity affected by the maiden order, a procession of Vestals crossed in front of the white horses, and not a man in Rome but would have trembled with superstitious awe at the bare notion of breaking in on the solemn march of these sacred virgins, dedicated to the service of a goddess, whose peculiar attributes were mystery, antiquity, and remorseless vengeance for offence.

Dressed in their long, white garments, simple and severe, with no relief save a narrow purple border round the veil, they swept on in slow, majestic column, like a vision from the other world, led by a stately priestess, pale and calm, of lofty stature and majestic bearing. They believed that to them was confided the welfare of the state, the safety of the city; nay, that with the mysterious symbols in their temple, they guarded the very existence of the nation; therefore on all public occasions of strife or disorder, the Vestal Virgins were accustomed to show themselves confidently in the streets, and use their influence for the restoration of peace. Nor had they need to fear either injury or insult. To touch the person of a Vestal, even to obstruct the litter in which she was carried, was punishable with death, and public opinion in such a case was even more exacting than the law. Immunities and privileges of many kinds were granted to the order by different enactments. When the Vestal went abroad, she was preceded and followed by the lictors of the State; and if she met a criminal under sentence of death, honestly by accident, during her progress, he was pardoned and set free for her sake, on the spot.

It may be that Mariamne had some vague recollection of this custom, for no sooner were the horses stopped to let the procession pass, than she uttered a loud shriek, which brought it to a halt at once, and caused her own guards to gather round the chariot, and prepare for resistance, Oarses wisely keeping aloof, and Damasippus, while he strove to wear a bold front, quaking in every limb.

At a signal from the superior priestess, the long, white line stood still, while her lictors seized the horses, and surrounded the chariot. Already a crowd of curious bystanders was gathering, and the glare of the burning Capitol shed its light even here, on their dark, eager faces, contrasting strangely with the veiled figures that occupied the middle of the street, cold and motionless as marble.

Two lictors seized on Damasippus, each by a

shoulder, and brought him unceremoniously to within a few paces of the priestess. Here he dropped upon his knees, and began wringing his hands in ludicrous dismay, whilst the populace, gathering round, laughed and jeered at him, only refraining from violence on account of the Vestal's presence.

"She is a slave, our slave, bought with our own money in the market, sacred virgin. I can swear it. I can prove it. Here is the man who paid for her. Oh! accursed Oarses, hast thou left me in the lurch at last?"

The wily Egyptian now came up, composed and sedate, with the air of a man confident in the justice of his cause. Mariamne, meanwhile, could but strive to release herself in vain. So effectually had she been bound and muffled, that she could scarcely move, and was unable to articulate. She struggled on, nevertheless, in the wild hope of succour, writhing her whole body to set her lips free from the bandages that stifled them.

With the quiet dignity which was an especial attribute of her office, the priestess pointed to the chariot containing the prisoner, and from beneath her veil, in clear, low tones, while the bystanders listened with respectful awe, came the question—

"What crime has she committed?"

"No crime, sacred virgin, no crime whatsoever," replied the wily Oarses, well knowing that the privilege of pardon, which the Vestals loved to exercise, was less likely to be exerted for a refractory bondswoman than a condemned criminal. "She is but a runaway slave, a mere dancing-girl. How shall I tell it in your august presence? I bought her scarce a week ago, as my friend here knows, and can swear. Canst thou not, Damasippus, worthy citizen? I gave but two thousand sesterces, nevertheless it was a large sum for me, who am a poor man; and I borrowed the half of it from my friend here. I bought her in the open market, and I took her home with me to my wife and children, that she might beat flax and card wool, and so gain an honest livelihood—an honest livelihood, sacred virgin; and that is why she ran away from me; so I informed the ædile, and I sought her diligently, and to-day I found her with her cheeks painted, and her bosom gilt, in her old haunts, drunk with wine. Then I bound her, and placed her in a litter, and the litter breaking down, for I am poor, sacred virgin, and of humble birth, though a Roman citizen,—the litter, I say, breaking down, and my patron's chariot passing by, I placed her within it, that I might take her home, for she is insensible still. All this I swear, and here is my friend who will swear it too. Damasippus, wilt thou not?"

The latter worthy had indeed been accompanying every syllable of his confederate's statement with those eager Italian gestures which signify so much of argument and expostulation. These were not without effect on the bystanders, predisposed as such generally are to believe the worst, and prone to be influenced by the last speaker, especially when supported by testimony, however unworthy of reliance. They crowded in as near as their awe of the priestess would allow, and angry looks were shot at the poor, dark figure lying helpless in the chariot.

Under the Vestal's long white veil, there might have been a gleam of pity or a flash of scorn on the unseen face, according as she felt a kindly sympathy, or womanly indignation for the sins of an erring sister. But whatever was her private opinion, with a priestess of her order, such an appeal as that of Oarses could have but one result. The pale, slender hand made a gesture of contempt and impatience. The tall, ghostly figure moved on with a prouder, sterner step, and the procession swept by, carrying away with it the last fragile hope of succour that had comforted Mariamne's heart.

Like a poor hunted hind caught in a net, when the sharp muzzle of the deer-hound touches her flank, the Jewess made one convulsive effort that loosened the shawl about her mouth. In her agony, the beloved name flew instinctively to her lips, and hopelessly, unconsciously, she called out, "Esca! Esca!" in loud piercing tones of terror and despair.

The Vestals had, indeed, passed by, and the chariot was again set in motion, but the Briton's name seemed to act as a talisman on the crowd, for no sooner had she pronounced it, than the bystanders were seen to give way on each side to the pressure of a huge pair of shoulders, surmounted by the fearless, honest face of Hirpinus the gladiator.

That professional, in common with a few chosen comrades, had found the last few hours hang exceedingly heavy on his hands. Bound by oath to keep sober, and, what was perhaps even a more galling restriction, to abstain from fighting, this little party had seen themselves deprived at once of their two principal resources, the favourite occupations which gave a zest to their existence. But the saying that there is "Honour among thieves" dates further back than the institution of an amphitheatre; and as soon as the gladiator had made his bargain, he considered himself, body and soul, the property of his purchaser. So, when Hippias gave his final orders, insisting on the appearance of his myrmidons at a given place and a given time, fresh, sober, and without a scratch, he had no fear but that they would be punctually and honestly obeyed.

Accordingly, Hirpinus, Rufus, Lutorius, and a few of the surest blades in the Family, had been wiling away their leisure with a stroll through the principal streets of Rome, and had met with not a few incidents peculiarly pleasing to men of their profession. They had been good enough to express their approval of the soldierlike manner in which the gardens of Sallust were attacked and carried; they had also marked, with a certain grim satisfaction, the assault on the Capitol, though they complained that when it was fired, the thick volumes of smoke, that swept downward from its walls, obstructed their view of the fighting, which was to them the chief attraction of the entertainment, and which they criticized with many instructive and professional remarks; it was difficult, doubtless, to abstain from taking part in any of these skirmishes, more particularly as each man was armed with the short two-edged Roman sword; but, as they reminded one another, it was only a temporary abstinence, and for a very short period, since, from all they could gather, before midnight they might be up to their necks in wine, and over their ankles in blood.

Now, supper-time was approaching, and the athletes were getting fierce, hungry, and weary of inaction. They had stood still to watch the procession of Vestals pass by, and even these wild, unscrupulous men had refrained from word or gesture that could be construed into disrespect for the maiden order; but they had shown little interest in the cause of stoppage, and scarce condescended to notice a discussion that arose from so mean a subject as a runaway slave. Suddenly, however, to the amazement of his comrades, and the discomfiture of the bystanders, Hirpinus burst hastily through the crowd, unceremoniously thrusting aside those who stood in his way, and lifting one inquisitive little barber clean off his legs, to hurl him like a plaything into a knot of chattering citizens, much to their indignation, and the poor man's own physical detriment. Hands were clenched, indeed, and brows bent, as the strong, square form forged through the press, like some bluff galley through the surf, but "*Cave*," "*Cave*," was whispered by the more cautious, and in such dread was a gladiator held by his peaceful fellow-citizens, that the boldest preferred submission under insult, to a quarrel with a man whose very trade was strife.

The chariot was already in motion, when a strong hand forced the two centre horses back upon their haunches, and the bold, frank voice of Hirpinus was heard above the trampling hoofs and general confusion.

"Easy, my little fellow, for a moment," said he to the indignant Automedon. "I heard a comrade's name spoken just now, from within that gilded shell of thine. Halt! I tell thee, lad, and keep that whip quiet, lest I brain thee with my open hand!"

Automedon, little relishing the business from the beginning, pulled his horses together, and looked very much disposed to cry.

Damasippus, however, confident in the support of his companion, and the presence of half a dozen armed slaves, stepped boldly forward, and bade the gladiator "Make way there" in a high, authoritative voice.

Hirpinus recognized the freedman at once, and laughed loud and long.

"What now?" said he, "my old convive and boon-companion. By Pollux! I knew thee not in thy warlike array of steel. In faith, a garland of roses becomes that red nose of thine better than the bosses of a helmet, and the stem of a goblet would fit thy hand more deftly than the haft of that gaudy sword. What stolen goods are these, old parasite? I'll wager now that the jackal is but taking home a lump of carrion to the lion's den."

"Stay me not, good friend," replied the other, with importance. "It is even as you say, and I am about the business of your employer and mine, Julius Placidus, the Tribune."

Hirpinus, in high good-humour, would have bade him pass on, but Mariamne, whose mouth was now released, gathered her exhausted energies for a last appeal.

"You are his comrade! you said so even now. Save me, save me, for Esca's sake!"

Again at that name the gladiator's eye glistened. He loved the young Briton like a son—he who had so little to love in the world. He had brought him out, as he boasted twenty times a day. He had made a man,—more, a swordsman,—of him. Now he had lost sight of him, and, as far as his nature permitted, had been anxious and unhappy ever since. If a dog had belonged to Esca, he would have dashed in to rescue it from danger at any risk.

"Stand back, fool!" he shouted to Damasippus, as the latter interposed his person between the gladiator and the chariot. "Have a care, I tell thee! I want the woman out into the street. What! you will, will you?—One—Two.—Take it then, idiot! Here! comrades, close in, and keep off this accursed crowd!"

Damasippus, confident in the numbers of his escort, and believing, too, that his adversary was alone, had, indeed, drawn his sword, and called up the slaves to his assistance, when the gladiator moved towards the chariot containing his charge. To dash the blade from his unaccustomed grasp, to deal him a straight, swift, crushing blow, that sent him down senseless on the pavement, and then, drawing his own weapon, to turn upon the shrinking escort a point that seemed to threaten all at once, was for Hirpinus a mere matter of professional business, so simple as to be almost a relaxation. His comrades, laughing boisterously, made a ring round the combatants. The slaves hesitated, gave ground, turned and fled; Hirpinus dragged the helpless form of Mariamne from the chariot, and Oarses, who had remained in the background till now, leaped nimbly in, to assume the vacant place, and whispering Automedon, went off at a gallop.

The poor girl, terrified by the danger she had escaped, and scarcely reassured by the mode of her rescue, or the appearance of her deliverers, clung, half-fainting, to the person of her supporter, and the old swordsman, with a delicacy almost ludicrous in one of his rough exterior, soothed her with such terms of encouragement as he could summon at the moment; now like a nurse hushing a child off to sleep, anon like a charioteer quieting a frightened or fretful horse.

In the meantime, the crowd, gathering confidence from the sheathed swords and obvious good-humour of the gladiators, pressed round with many rude gestures and insulting remarks, regardless of the fallen man, who, on recovering his senses, wisely remained for a while where he was, and chiefly bent on examining the features of the cloaked and hooded prize, that had created this pretty little skirmish for their diversion. Such unmannerly curiosity soon aroused the indignation of Hirpinus.

"Keep them off, comrades!" said he, angrily; "these miserable citizens. Keep them off, I say! Have they never seen a veiled woman before, that they gape and stare, and pass their rancid jests, as they do on you and me when we are down on our backs for their amusement in the arena? Let her have air, my lads, and she will soon come to. Pollux! She looks like the lily thy wife was watering at home, when we stopped there this morning, Rufus, for a draught of the five-year-old wine, and a gambol with those bright-haired kids of thine."

The tall champion to whom this remark was addressed, and who had that very morning, in company with his friend, bidden a farewell that might be eternal, to wife and children, as indeed it was nothing unusual for him to do, softened doubtless by the remembrance, now exerted himself strenuously to give the fainting woman room. Without the use of any but nature's weapons, and from sheer weight, strength, and resolution, the gladiators soon cleared an ample space in the middle of the street for their comrade and his charge; nor did they seem at all indisposed to a task which afforded opportunities of evincing their own physical superiority, and the supreme contempt in which they held the mass of their fellow-citizens.

Perhaps it was pleasant to feel how completely they could domineer over the crowd by the use of those very qualities which made their dying struggles a spectacle for the vulgar; perhaps they enjoyed the repayment in advance of some of the ribaldry and insult that would too surely accompany their end. At any rate they shouldered the mob back with unnecessary violence, drove their spiked sandals into the feet of such as came under their tread, and scrupled not to strike with open hand or clenched fist any adventurous citizen who was fool enough to put himself forward for appeal or resistance.

These, too, seemed terrorstricken by this handful of resolute men. Accustomed to look on them from a safe distance in the amphitheatre, like the wild beasts with whom they often saw them fight, they were nearly as unwilling to beard the one as the other; and to come into collision with a gladiator in the street, was like meeting a tiger on the wrong side of his bars.

So Hirpinus had plenty of room to undo the girl's bands, and remove the stifling folds that muffled her head and throat.

"Where am I?" she murmured, as she began to breathe more freely, looking round bewildered and confused. "You are Esca's friend. Surely I heard you say so. You will take care of me, then, for Esca's sake."

Instinctively she addressed herself to Hirpinus, instinctively she seemed to appeal to him for protection and encouragement.

The veil had been taken from her head, and the beauty of the sweet pale face was not lost on the surrounding gladiators.

Old Hirpinus looked at her with a comical expression, in which admiration and pity were blended with astonishment and a proud sense of personal appropriation in the defenceless girl who seemed utterly dependent on him. He had never seen anything so beautiful in his life. He had never known the happiness of a home; never had wife or child, but at that moment his heart warmed to her as a father's to a daughter.

"Where are you," he repeated, "pretty flower?

You are within a hundred paces of the Flaminian Way. How came you here? Ay, that is more than I can tell you. Yonder knave lying there.—What? he is gone, is he? Ay! I *could* not hit hard enough at a man with whom I have emptied so many skins of Sabine.—Well, Damasippus brought thee here, he best knows why, in his master's gaudy chariot. I heard thee squeak, my pretty one, and who loves Esca, loves me, and I love him, or her, or whoever it may be. So I knocked him over, that fat freedman, and took thee from the chariot, and pulled off these wraps that were stifling thee, and indeed I think it was about time."

He had raised her while he spoke, and supported her on his strong arm, walking slowly on, while the gladiators closing round them, moved steadily along the street, followed, though at a safe distance, by much verbal insult and abuse. At intervals, two or three of the rear-guard would turn and confront the mob, who immediately gave back and were silent. Thus the party proceeded on its way, more, it would seem, with the view of leaving the crowd than of reaching any definite place of shelter.

"Where are we going? and who are those who

guard us?" whispered Mariamne, clinging close to her protector. "You will take care of me, will you not?" she added, in a confiding tone.

"They are my comrades," he answered, soothingly; "and old Hirpinus will guard you, pretty one, like the apple of his eye. We will take you straight home, or wherever you wish to go, and not one of these will molest you while I am by—never fear!"

Just then, Euchenor, who was one of the band, and had overheard this reassuring sentence, clapped the old swordsman on the shoulder.

"You seem to forget our compact," said he, with his evil, mocking laugh.

The face of Hirpinus fell, and his brow lowered, for he remembered then that Mariamne was not much better off here than in the captivity from which he had rescued her.

CHAPTER XI.

THE RULES OF THE FAMILY.

THE Jewess had indeed but escaped one danger to fall into another. Bold and lawless as were these professional swordsmen, they acknowledged certain rules of their own, which they were never known to infringe. When a band of gladiators had been mustered, and in military language "told off" for a particular service, it was their custom to bind themselves by oath, as forming one body, unanimous and undivisible, until that service was completed. They swore to stand by each other to the death, to obey their chief implicitly, and to take orders from him alone—to make common cause with their fellows, in defiance of all personal feelings of interest or danger, even to the cheerful sacrifice of life itself; and to consider all booty of arms, gold, jewels, captives, or otherwise, however obtained, as the property of the band; subject to its disposal, according to the established code of their profession.

Therefore it was, that Hirpinus felt his heart sink at Euchenor's malicious observation. Therefore it was, that though he strove to put on an appearance of good-humour and confidence, a perceptible tremor shook his voice while he replied—

"I found her first. I dragged her from the chariot. I put that foolish citizen on his back to make sport for you all. I am the oldest swordsman in the band. I think you might leave her to me!"

Euchenor's eye was on the frightened girl, and meeting its glance, she shrunk yet closer to her protector, while the Greek observed, with a sneer—

"You had better make a new set of rules for us then, since you seem inclined to break through the old. Comrades, I appeal to you; doth not the booty belong to us all, share and share alike?"

The others were crowding in now, having reached a narrower street and left the populace behind. "Of course, of course!" was re-echoed on all sides; "who doubts it? who disputes it?"

"What would you have, man?" exclaimed Hirpinus, waxing wrath. "You cannot cut a captive into twenty pieces and give every man a portion! I tell you, she is mine. Let her alone!"

"You cannot cut a wineskin into twenty pieces, nor need you," replied the Greek; "but you pass it round amongst your comrades, till every man's thirst be slaked. 'Faith, after that, you may keep the empty skin for your own share, if you like!"

He spoke in a cold, derisive tone, and although Mariamne could not understand half he said, garnished, as his speech was, with the cant terms of his calling, she gathered enough of its import to be terrified at the prospect before her.

Old Hirpinus lost patience at last.

"Will *you* take her from me?" he burst out, knitting his bushy brows, and putting his face close to the Greek's. "Stand up then like a man and *try!*"

Euchenor turned very pale. It was no part of his scheme to provoke his robust old comrade to a personal encounter; and, indeed, the pugilist was a coward at heart, owing his reputation chiefly to the skill with which he had always matched himself against those whom he was sure to conquer. Now he fell back a step or two from his glaring adversary, and appealed once more to their companions.

These gathered round, speaking all at once, Hirpinus turning from one to the other, and ever shielding his charge with his body, as an animal shields its young. He was determined to save the girl, because he understood dimly that she belonged in some way to Esca, and the loyal old swordsman would not have hesitated one moment in flinging his life down, then and there, to purchase her safety.

"Hold, comrades!" shouted he, in a stentorian voice that made itself heard above the din. "Will ye bay me altogether like a pack of Molossian wolf-hounds? Hounds, forsooth! nay, the Molossians are true-bred, and there is *one* cur amongst us here at least, to *my* knowledge. Rather, like a knot of jabbering old women in a market-place! Talk of rules! Of course we abide by our rules, ay, and stick to our oath. Rufus, old friend, we have stood with our swords at each other's throats for hours together, many a time during the last ten years, and never had an angry word, or an unkindly thought. Thou wilt not fail me now?—Thou wilt not see old Hirpinus wronged?"

The champion thus appealed to by such tender

associations, thrust his tall person forward in the throng. Slow of speech, calm, calculating, and reflective, Rufus was held an oracle of good sense amongst his fellow-swordsmen.

"You are both wrong," said he, sententiously. "The girl belongs to neither of you. If this had happened yesterday, Hirpinus would have had a right to carry her where he chose. But we have taken the oath since then, old comrade, and she is the joint property of the band by all our laws."

"I said so!" exclaimed Euchenor, triumphantly. "The prize belongs to us all. Every man his turn. The apple seems fair and ripe enough. Mine shall be the hand to pare its rind."

As he spoke, he pulled aside the veil which Mariamne had modestly drawn once more about her head, and the girl flushing scarlet at the insult, stamped passionately with her foot, and then, as if acknowledging her helplessness, burst into tears, and hid her face in her hands.

Hirpinus caught the aggressor by the shoulder, and sent him reeling back amongst the rest. His beard bristled with anger, and the foam stood on his lip like some old boar at bay.

"Hands off!" roared the veteran. "Rules or no rules, another such jest as that and I drive a foot of steel through the jester's brisket! What? Rufus, I came not into the Family yesterday. I was eating raw flesh and lentil porridge when most of these were sucking their mothers' milk. I tell thee, man, the old law was this:—When gladiators disputed on any subject whatever—pay, plunder, or precedence—they were to take short swords, throw away their shields, and fight it out by pairs, till they were agreed. Stand round, comrades! Put the little Greek up at half-sword distance; clear a space of seven feet square, not an inch more, and I'll show you how we used to settle these matters when Nero wore the purple!"

"Nay, nay!" interposed Mariamne, wringing her hands in an agony of terror and dismay. "Shed not blood on my account. I am a poor, helpless girl. I have done no one any harm. Let me go, for pity's sake. Let me go!"

But to this solution of the difficulty, objections were offered on all sides. Rufus indeed, and one or two of the older swordsmen, moved by the youth and tears of the captive, would willingly have permitted her to escape; but Euchenor, Lutorius, and the rest objected violently to the loss of so beautiful a prize. Rufus, too, when appealed to, though he would fain have supported his old comrade, was obliged to confess that justice, according to gladiator's law, was on Euchenor's side. Even the proposal to fight for her possession by pairs, popular as it was likely to be in such a company, was rendered inadmissible by the terms of the late oath. The band indeed, when purchased as they had been by Hippias, for a special duty to be performed that night, had become pledged according to custom, not only to the usual brotherhood and community of interests, but also to refrain from baring steel upon any pretence or provocation, either amongst themselves or against a common foe, until ordered to do so by their employer. Hirpinus, though he chafed and swore vehemently, and kept Mariamne close under his wing through it all, was obliged to acknowledge the force of his comrade's arguments; and the puzzled athlete racked his unaccustomed brains till his head ached, to find some means of escape for the girl he had resolved to save. In the meantime, delay was dangerous. These men were not used to hesitate or refrain, and already the hour was approaching at which they were to muster for their night's work, whatever it might be, in the Tribune's house. The old swordsman felt he must dissemble, were it but to gain time, so he smoothed his brows, and, much against the grain, assumed an appearance of good-humour and satisfaction.

"Be it as you will," said he, "old Hirpinus is the last man to turn round upon his comrades, or to break the laws of the Family, for the sake of a cream-coloured face and a wisp of black hair. I will abide by the decision of Hippias. We shall find him at the Tribune's house, and it is time we were there now. Forward, my lads! Nay, hands off! I tell thee once more, Euchenor, till we have brought her to the master's, she belongs to me."

Euchenor grumbled, but was compelled to submit, for the other's influence amongst the gladiators was far greater than his own. And the little party, with Mariamne in the centre, still clinging fast to Hirpinus, moved on in the direction of the Tribune's house.

Esca crouching in his place of concealment, silent and wary, as he had oft-times crouched long ago, when watching for the dun-deer on the hill-side, was aware of the tramp of disciplined men approaching the porch in which he lay in ambush. Every faculty was keenly, painfully on the stretch. Once, at the sound of wheels, he had started from his lair, ready to make one desperate attempt for the rescue of his love; but greatly to his consternation, the gilded chariot returned empty, save of Automedon, looking much scared and bewildered. The wily Oarses indeed, having made his escape from the gladiators, had betaken himself to his lodging, and there determined to remain, either till his patron's wrath should be exhausted, or till the events which he foresaw the night would bring forth, should have diverted it into another channel. So Automedon went home in fear and trembling by himself. As the Briton revolved matters in his mind, he knew not whether to be most alarmed or reassured by this unforeseen contingency. Though the chariot had returned without Mariamne, the freedmen and armed slaves were still absent. Could they have missed their prey, and were they still searching for her? or had they carried her elsewhere?—to the freedmen's garret perhaps, there to remain concealed, till the night was further advanced. Yet the words of Placidus, or of his ghost, which he had overheard, seemed to infer that the Jewess was expected every minute. Every minute indeed! and those racking minutes seemed to stretch themselves to hours. With the natural impatience of inaction, which accompanies uncertainty, he had almost made up his mind to return in search of Eleazar, when the steady footfall of the approaching party arrested his attention.

There was a bright moon shining above, and the open space into which the gladiators advanced was clear as day. With a keen feeling of confidence he recognized the square frame of Hirpinus, and then, as he caught sight of the dark-robed figure at the swordsman's side, for one exulting moment, doubt, fear, anxiety, all were merged in the delight of seeing Mariamne once more.

With the bound of a wild deer, he was in the midst of them, clasping her in his arms, and the girl sobbing on his breast, felt safe and happy, because she was with *him*.

Hirpinus gave a shout that startled the slaves laying the tables in the inner hall.

"Safe, my lad!" he exclaimed, "and in a whole skin. Sound and hearty, and fit to join us in to-night's work. Better late than never. Swear him, comrades! swear him on the spot! Send in for a morsel of bread and a pinch of salt. Here, Rufus, cross thy blade with mine! Thou art in the nick of time, lad, to take thy share with the rest, of peril, and pleasure, and profit to boot!"

This speech he eked out with many winks and

signs to his young friend, for Hirpinus, guessing how matters stood between the pair, could think of no better plan by which Esca should at least claim a share in the prey they had so recently acquired.

His artifice was, however, lost upon the Briton, who seemed wholly occupied with Mariamne, and to whom the girl was whispering her fears and distresses, and entreaties that he would save her from the band.

The young man drew her to his side. "Give way," said he, haughtily, as Euchenor and Lutorius closed in upon him. "She has made her choice, she goes with me. I take her home to her father's house."

The others set up a shout of derision. "Hear him!" they cried. "It is the Prætor who speaks! It is the voice of Cæsar himself! Yes, yes, go in peace, if thou wilt. We have had enough and to spare of your yellow-haired barbarians, but the girl remains with us."

She was not trembling now. She was past all fear in such a crisis as this. Erect and defiant she stood beside her champion, pale indeed as the dead, but with eyes in which flashed the courage of despair.

His lips were white with the effort of self-command as he strove to keep cool and to use fair words.

"I am one of yourselves," said he. "You will not turn against me all at once. Let me but take the maiden home, and I will come back and join you, true as the blade to the haft."

"Ay, let them go!" put in Hirpinus. "He speaks fairly, and these barbarians never fail their word!"

"No, no," interposed Euchenor. "He has nothing to do with us. Why, he was beaten in the open Circus by a mere patrician. Besides, he is not engaged for to-night. He has no interest in the job. Who is he, this barbarian, that we should give up to him the fairest prize we are like to take in the whole business?"

"Will you fight for her?" thundered Esca, hitching his sword-belt to the front.

Euchenor shrank back amongst his comrades. "Our oath forbids me," said he; and the others, though they could not refrain from jeering at the unwilling Greek, confirmed his decision.

Esca's mind was made up. "Pass your hands under my girdle," he whispered to Mariamne. "Hold fast, and we shall break through!"

His sword was out like lightning, and he dashed amongst the gladiators, but he had to do with men thoroughly skilled in arms and trained to every kind of personal contest.

A dozen blades were gleaming in the moonlight as ready as his own. A dozen points were threatening him, backed by fearless hearts, and strong, supple, practised hands. He was at bay, a desperate man penned in by a circle of steel. He glanced fiercely round, defiant yet bewildered, then down at the pale face at his breast, and his heart sank within him. He was at his wits' end.

She looked up,—loving, resolute, and courageous. "Dear one," she said, softly, "let me rather die by your hand. See, I do not fear. Strike! You only have the right, for I am yours!"

Even then a faint blush came into her cheek, while the pale hands busied themselves with her dress to bare her bosom for the blow.

He turned his point upon her, and she smiled up in his face. Old Hirpinus dashed the tears from his shaggy eyelashes.

"Hold! Hold!" said he, in a broken voice. "Not till I am down and out of the game for one! Enough of this!" he added in an altered tone and with a ludicrous assumption of his usual careless manner. "Here comes the master—no more wrangling, lads! we will refer the matter to him!"

While he spoke, Hippías entered the open space in front of the Tribune's house, and the gladiators gathered eagerly around him, Euchenor alone remaining somewhat in the background.

CHAPTER XII.

A MASTER OF FENCE.

HIPPIAS knew well how to maintain discipline amongst his followers. While he interested himself keenly in their training and personal welfare, he permitted no approach to familiarity, and above all never suffered a syllable of discussion on a command, or a moment's hesitation in its fulfilment. He came now to put himself at their head for the carrying out of a hazardous and important enterprise. The consciousness of coming danger, especially when it is of a kind with which habit has rendered him familiar, and which practice has taught him to baffle by his own skill and courage, has a good moral effect on a brave man's character. It cheers his spirits, it exalts his imagination, it sharpens his intellects, and, above all, it softens his heart. Hippias felt that to-night he would need all the qualities he most prized to carry him safely through his task—that while failure must be inevitable destruction, success would open out to him a career of which the ultimate goal might be a procuratorship or even a kingdom. How quickly past, present, and possible future flitted through his brain! It was not so long since his first victory in the amphitheatre! He remembered, as if it were but yesterday, the canvas awnings, the blue sky, and the confused mass of faces, framing that dazzling sweep of sand, all of which his sight took in at once, though his eyes were fixed on those of the watchful Gaul, whom he disarmed in a couple of passes, and slew without the slightest remorse. He could feel again, even now, the hot breath of the Libyan tiger, as he fell beneath it, choked with sand and covered by his buckler, stabbing desperately at that sinewy chest in which the life seemed to lie so deep. The tiger's claws had left their marks upon his brawny shoulder, but he had risen from the contest victorious, and Red and Green through the whole crowded building, from the senators' cushions to the slaves' six inches of standing-room, cheered him to a man. After this triumph who such a favourite with the Roman people as handsome Hippias? Again, he was the centre of all observation, as, confessedly the head of his profession, he set in order Nero's cruel shows, and catered with profuse splendour for the tastes of Imperial Rome. Yes, he had reached the pinnacle of a gladiator's fame, and from that elevation a prospect opened itself that he had scarcely even dreamed of till now. A handful of determined men, a torch or two for every score of blades, a palace in flames, a night of blood (he only hoped and longed that there might be resistance enough to distinguish strife from murder), another dynasty, a grateful patron, and a brave man's services worthily acknowledged and repaid. Then the future would indeed smile in gorgeous hues. Which of Rome's dominions in the east would most fully satisfy the thirst for royal luxury that he now experienced for the first time? In which of his manlier qualities was he so inferior to the Jew, that Hippias the gladiator should make a lowlier monarch than Herod the Great? and men had not done talking of that warlike king, even now!—his wisdom, his cruelty, his courage, his splendour, and his crimes.

A Roman province was but another name for an independent government. Hippias saw himself enthroned in the blaze of majesty under a glowing eastern sky. Life offering all it had to give of pomp and pageantry and rich material enjoyment. Slaves, horses, jewels, banquets, dark-eyed women, silken eunuchs, and gaudy guards with burnished helmets and flashing shields of gold. Nothing wanting, not even one with whom to share the glittering vision. Valeria would be his. Valeria was born to be a queen. It would indeed be a triumph to offer the half of a throne to the woman, who had hitherto condescended by listening to his suit. There was a leavening of generosity in Hippias that caused him to reflect with intense pleasure on the far deeper homage he would pay her after so romantic a consummation of his hopes. He felt as if he could almost love her then, with the love he had experienced in his boyhood—that boyhood which seemed now to have been another's rather than his own. He had put it away long since, and it had not come back to him for years till to-day; but gratified vanity, the pleasure which most hearts experience in grasping an object that has been dangling out of reach, beyond all, the power, exerted by a woman, over one who has been accustomed to consider himself, either above or below such pleasing influences, had softened him strangely, and he hardly felt like the same man who made his bargain with the Tribune for a certain quantity of flesh and blood and mettle, so short a time ago.

It is not to be thought, however, that in his dreams of the future, the fencing-master neglected the means by which that future was to be attained. He had mustered and prepared his band with more than common care—had seen with his own eyes that their arms were bright and sharp and fit for work—had placed them at their appointed posts and visited them repeatedly, enjoining, above all things, extreme vigilance and sobriety. Not one of those men saw beneath his unruffled brow and quiet stern demeanour anything unusual in the conduct of their leader; not one could have guessed that schemes of ambition far beyond any he had ever cherished before, were working in his brain—that a strange, soft, kindly feeling was nestling at his heart.

He stood in the moonlight amongst his followers, calm, abrupt, severe as usual; and when

Hirpinus looked into his stern set face, the hopes of the old gladiator fell as did his countenance, but Mariamne perceived at once with a woman's eye something that taught her an appeal to his pity on this occasion would not be made in vain.

With habitual caution, his first proceeding was to count the band ere he took note of the two figures in their centre. Then he cast a scrutinizing glance at their arms to satisfy himself all were ready for immediate action. After that he turned with a displeased air to Hirpinus, and asked—

"What doth the woman amongst us? You heard my orders this morning. Who brought her here?"

Half a dozen voices were raised at once to answer the master's question; only he to whom it was especially addressed kept silence, knowing the nature with which he had to do.

Hippias raised but his sheathed sword and the clamour ceased. Not a maniple in all Rome's well-drilled legions seemed in better discipline than this handful of desperate men. Then he turned to Esca, still speaking in short incisive tones.

"Briton!" said he. "You are not one of us to-night. Go your ways in peace!"

"Well said!" shouted the gladiators. "He is no comrade of ours! He hath no share in our spoil!"

But Hippias only wished to save the Briton from the perils of the coming night, and this from some vague feeling he could hardly explain to himself, that Valeria was interested in the stalwart barbarian. It was not in the fencing-master's nature to entertain sentiments of jealousy upon uncertain grounds. And he was just fond enough of Valeria to value any one she liked for her sake. Moreover Esca knew their plans. He would alarm the palace and there would be a fight. He wished nothing better.

Esca was about to make his appeal, but Mariamne interposed.

"Where he goeth I will go," said she, almost in the words of her own sacred writings. "I have to-night lost father, and home, and people. This is the second time he hath saved me from captivity worse than death. Part us not now, I beseech thee, part us not!"

Hippias looked kindly on the sweet face with its large imploring eager eyes. "You love him," said he, "foolish girl. Begone then, and take him with you."

But again a fierce murmur rose amongst the gladiators. Not even the master's authority was sufficient to carry out such a breach of all laws and customs as this. Euchenor, ever prone to wrangle, stepped forward from the background, where he had remained so as to appear an impartial and uninterested observer.

"The oath!" exclaimed the Greek. "The oath —we swore it when the sun was up—shall we break it ere the moon goes down? She is ours, Hippias, by all the laws of the Family, and we will not give her up."

"Silence!" thundered the master, with a look that made Euchenor shrink back once more. "Who asked *you* for your vote? Hirpinus, Rufus, once again, how came this woman here?"

"She was bound hand and foot in a chariot," answered the former, ignoring, however, with less than his usual frankness, to whom that chariot belonged. "She was carried away by force. I protected her from ill-usage," he added stoutly, "as I would protect her again."

The girl gave him a grateful look, which sank into the old swordsman's heart. Esca, too, muttered warm broken words of thanks, while the band assented to the truth of this statement.

"Even so!" they exclaimed. "Hirpinus speaks well. That is why she belongs to us, and we claim every man his share."

Hippias was too experienced a commander not to know that there are times when it is necessary to yield with a good grace, and to use artifice if force will not avail. It is thus the skilful rider rules his steed, and the judicious wife her husband—the governing power in either case inducing the governed to believe that it obeys entirely of its own free will. He smiled therefore pleasantly on his followers, and addressed them in careless, good-humoured tones.

"She belongs to us all without doubt," said he, "and, by the sandals of Aphrodité, she is so fair that I shall put in my claim with the rest! Nevertheless there is no time to be wasted now, for the sake of the brightest eyes that ever flashed beneath a veil. Put her aside for a few hours or so. You, Hirpinus, as you captured her, shall take care that she does not escape. For the Briton we may as well keep him safe too—we may find a use for those long arms of his when to-night's business is accomplished. In the meantime, fall in, my heroes, and make ready for your work. Supper first (and it's laid even now) with the noblest patrician and the deepest drinker in Rome, Julius Placidus the Tribune!"

"*Euge!*" exclaimed the gladiators in a breath, forgetful at the moment of their recent dissatisfaction, and eager to hear more of the night's enterprise, about which they entertained the wildest and most various anticipations; nothing loth, besides, to share the orgies of a man whose table was celebrated for its luxuries amongst all classes in Rome.

Hippias looked round on their well-pleased faces, and continued:

"Then what say you, my children, to a walk through the palace gardens? We will take our swords, by Hercules, for the German guards are stubborn dogs, and best convinced by the argument each of us carries at his belt. It may be dark too ere we get there, for the moon is early to-night, and we have no need to stir till we have tasted the Tribune's wine, so we must not forget a few torches to light us on our way. There are a score at least lying ready in the corner of that porch. So we will join our comrades in a fair midnight frolic under Cæsar's roof. Cæsar's, forsooth! my children, there will be a smouldering palace and another Cæsar by to-morrow!"

"*Euge!*" exclaimed the gladiators once more.

"Hail, Cæsar! Long live Cæsar!" they repeated, with shouts of fierce mocking laughter.

"It is well," remarked Rufus, sagaciously, when silence was restored. "The pay is good and the work no heavier than an ordinary prætor's show. But I remember a fiercer lion than common, that Nero turned loose upon us once in the arena, and we called him 'Cæsar' amongst ourselves, because he was dangerous to meddle with. If the old man's purple is to be rent, we should have something over the regular pay. They have not lasted long of late, but still Hippias, 'tis somewhat out of the usual business. We don't change an emperor every night even now."

"True enough," answered the master, good-humouredly. "And you have never been within the walls of a palace in your life. Something beyond your pay, said you? Why, man, the pay is but a pretext, a mere matter of form. Once in Cæsar's chambers, a large-fisted fellow like Rufus here, may carry away a king's ransom in either hand. Then think of the old wine! Fifty year old Cæcuban, in six-quart cups of solid gold, and welcome to take the goblet away with you, besides, if you care to be encumbered with it. Shawls from Persia, lying about for mere coverings to the couches. Mother-of-pearl and ivory gleaming in every corner. Jewels scattered in heaps upon the floor. Only get the work done first, and every man here shall help himself unquestioned, and walk home with whatever pleases him best."

It was not often Hippias treated his followers to so long a speech, or one, in their estimation, so much to the purpose. They marked their approval with vehement and repeated shouts. They ceased to think of Esca, and forgot all about Mariamne and their late dissatisfaction; nay, they seemed now but to be impatient of every subject unconnected with their enterprise, and to grudge every minute that delayed them from their promised spoil. At a signal from Hippias, and his intimation that supper was ready, and their host awaiting them, they rushed tumultuously through the porch, leaving behind them Mariamne and Esca, guarded only by old Hirpinus and Euchenor, the latter appearing alone to be unmoved by the glowing prospects of plunder held out, and obstinately standing on his rights, determined not to lose sight of the captured girl, the more so that she was now overlooked by the rest of his comrades.

This man, though deficient in the dashing physical daring which is so popular a quality amongst those of his profession, possessed, nevertheless, a dogged tenacity of purpose, totally unqualified by any moral scruples or feelings of shame, which rendered him formidable as an antagonist, and generally successful in any villany he attempted.

As in the combats he waged with or without the heavy, lacerating cestus, his object was to tire out his adversary by protracted and scientific defence, taking as little punishment as possible, and never hazarding a blow, save when it could not be returned, so in everything he undertook, it was his study to reach the goal by unrelaxing vigilance, and unremitting recourse to the means which experience and common sense pointed out for its attainment.

Slinking behind the broad back of Hirpinus, he concealed himself in the darkest corner of the porch, and watched the result of Mariamne's appeal to the fencing-master.

Hippias pushed the gladiators on before him,

with boisterous good-humour, and considerable violence; as they crowded through the narrow entrance, he remained behind for a moment, and whispered to Esca—

"You will take the girl home, comrade. Can I trust you?"

"Trust me!" was all the Briton answered, but the tone in which he spoke, and the glance he exchanged with Mariamne, might have satisfied a more exacting inquirer than the captain of gladiators.

"Fare thee well, lad," said Hirpinus, "and thee, too, my pretty flower. I would go with you myself, but it is a long way from here to Tiber-side, and I must not be missing to-night, come what may."

"Begone, both of you!" added Hippias, hurriedly. "Had it not been for the plunder, I should scarce have found my lambs so reasonable to-night: were you to fall in with them again, the Vestals themselves could not save you. Begone, and farewell."

They obeyed and hastened off, while the fencing-master, with a well-pleased smile, clapped Hirpinus on the shoulder, and accompanied him into the house.

"Old comrade," said he, "we will drink a measure of the Tribune's Cæcuban to-night, come what may. To-morrow we shall either be on our backs, gaping for the death-fee, or pressing our lips to nothing meaner than a chalice of burnished gold. Who knows? Who cares?"

"Not I for one," replied Hirpinus; "but I am strangely thirsty in the meantime, and the Tribune's wine, they tell me, is the best in Rome."

CHAPTER XIII.

THE ESQUILINE.

WITH attentive ears, and faculties keenly on the stretch, Euchenor, lurking in the corner of the porch, listened to the foregoing conversation. When he gathered that Tiber-side was the direction the fugitives meant to take, his quick Greek intellect formed its plan of operation at once.

There was a post of his comrades, consisting of some of the gladiators purchased by Placidus, and placed there a few hours since by the orders of Hippias, in the direct road for that locality.

He would follow the pair, noiseless and unsuspected, for he had no mind to provoke an encounter with the Briton, till within reach of assistance, then give the alarm, seize the wayfarers, and appeal to the club-law they all held sacred, for his rights. Esca would be sure to defend the girl with his life, but he would be overpowered by numbers, and it would be strange if he could not be quieted for ever in the struggle. There would still be time enough, thought Euchenor, after his victory to join his comrades at the Tribune's table, leaving the girl to the tender mercies of the band. He could make some excuse for his absence to satisfy his companions, heated as they would by that time be with wine. Indeed, for his own part, he had no great fancy for the night's adventure, promising as it did more hard knocks than he cared to exchange in a fight with the German guard, fierce blue-eyed giants, who would give and take no quarter. He did not wish, indeed, to lose his share of the plunder, for no one was more alive to the advantages of a full purse, but he trusted to his own dexterity for securing this, without running unnecessary risk. Meanwhile, it was his method to attend to one thing at a time; he waited impatiently, therefore, till Hippias entered the house, and left him at liberty to emerge from his hiding-place.

No sooner was the master's back turned, than the Greek sped into the street, glancing eagerly down its long vista lying white in the moonlight, for the two dark figures he sought. Agile and noiseless as a panther, he skulked swiftly along under the shadow of the houses, till he reached the corner which a passenger would turn who was bound for Tiber-side. Here he made sure that he must sight his prey; but no, amongst the few wayfarers who dotted this less solitary district he looked in vain for Esca's towering shoulders or the shrinking figure of the Jewess. In vain, like a hound, he quested to and fro, now casting forward upon a vague speculation, now trying back with untiring perseverance and determination. Like a hound, too, whose game has foiled him, he was obliged to slink home at length, ashamed and baffled, to the porch of the Tribune's house, inventing as he went a plausible excuse to host and comrades for his tardy appearance at the banquet. He had passed, nevertheless, within twenty paces of those he hunted, but he knew it not.

With the first rapture of intense joy for their escape, it was in the nature of Mariamne that her predominant feeling should be one of gratitude to heaven for thus preserving both herself and him whose life was dearer to her than her own. In common with her nation, she believed in the constant and immediate interposition of the Almighty in favour of his servants, and the new faith, which was rapidly gaining ground in her heart, had tempered the awe in which his worshipper regards the Deity, with the implicit trust, and love, and confidence entertained for its father by a child. Such feelings can but find an outlet in thanksgiving and prayer. Before Mariamne had gone ten paces from the Tribune's house, she stopped short, looked up in Esca's face, and said, "Let us kneel together, and thank God for our deliverance."

"Not here at least!" exclaimed the Briton, whose nerves, good as they were, had been somewhat unstrung by the vicissitudes of the night, and the apprehensions that had racked him for his beloved companion. "They may return at any moment. You are not safe even now. If you are so exhausted you cannot go on (for she was leaning heavily on his arm, and her head drooped), I will carry you in my arms from here to your father's house. My love, I would carry you through the world."

She smiled sweetly on him, though her face was very pale. "Let us turn in at this ruined gateway," said she; "a few moments' rest will restore me, and Esca, I must give thanks to the God of Israel, who has saved both thee and me."

They were near a crumbling archway, with a broken iron gate that had fallen in. It was on the opposite side of the street to the Tribune's house; and as they passed beneath its mouldering span, they saw that it formed an entrance into one of those wildernesses, which, after the great fire of Nero, existed here and there, not only in the suburbs, but at the very heart of Rome.

They were, in truth, in that desolate waste which had once been the famous Esquiline Gardens, originally a burial-ground, and granted by Augustus to his favourite, the illustrious Mæcenas, to plant and decorate according to his prolific fancy and unimpeachable taste. That learned nobleman had taken advantage of his emperor's liberality, to build here a stately palace, which had not, however, escaped the great fire, and to lay out extensive pleasure-grounds, which had been devastated by the same calamity. Little, indeed, now remained, save the trees that had originally shadowed the Roman's grave in the days of the old republic. The "unwelcome cypresses" so touchingly described in his most reflective ode, by him whose genius Mæcenas fostered, and whose gratitude paid his princely patron back by rendering him immortal.

Many a time had Horace lounged in these pleasant shades, musing with quaint and varied fancies, half pathetic half grotesque, on the business and the pleasures, the sunshine and the shadows, the aim and the end, of that to him inexplicable problem, a man's short life. Here, too, perhaps, he speculated on the mythology, to the beauty of which his poetic imagination was so keenly alive, while his strong common sense and somewhat material character, must have been so utterly incredulous of its truth. Nay, on this very spot did he not ridicule certain superstitions of his countrymen, with a coarseness that is only redeemed by its wit? and preserve in pungent sarcasm, for coming ages, the memory of an indecent statue on the Esquiline, as he has preserved in sweet and glowing lines, the glades of cool Præneste, or the terraced vineyards basking in the glare and glitter of noonday on Tibur's sunny slopes? Here, perhaps, many a time may have been seen the stout, sleek form, so round and well-cared for, with its clean white gown, and dainty shining head, crowned with a garland of festive roses, and not wanting, be sure, a festive goblet in its hand. Here may the poet have sat out many a joyous hour in the shade, with mirth, and song, and frequent sips of old Falernian, and a vague, dreary fancy the while, ever present, though unacknowledged—like a death's head at the banquet—that feast, and jest, and song could not last for ever, but that the time must come at length, when the empty jar would not be filled again, when the faded roses could be bound together no longer in a chaplet for the unconscious brows, and the string of the lyre once snapped, must be silent henceforward for evermore.

The very waterfall that had soothed its master to his noonday slumber in the drowsy shade, was now dried up, and in the cavity above, a heap of dusty rubbish alone remained, where erst the cool, translucent surface shone, fair and smooth as glass. Weeds were growing rank and tall, where once the myrtle quivered and the roses bloomed. Where Chloe gambolled and where Lydia sang, the raven croaked and fluttered, and the night-owl screamed. Instead of velvet turf, and trim exotic shrubs, and shapely statues framed in bowers of green, the nettle spread its festering carpet, and the dock put out its pointed leaf, and here and there a tombstone showed its slab of marble, smooth and grim, like a bone that has been laid bare. All was ruin or decay—a few short years had done the work of ages; and whether they waked or whether they slept, poet and patron had gone hence, never to return.

Under the branches of a spectral holm-oak, blackened, withered, and destroyed by fire, Mariamne paused, and clung with both hands to her companion's arm. Bravely had the girl borne up for hours against terrible mental anxiety, as well as actual bodily pain, but with relief and comparative safety came the reaction. Her eyes grew dim, her senses seemed failing, and her limbs trembled so that she was unable to proceed.

He hung over her in positive fear. The pale face looked so death-like that his bold heart quailed, as the possibility presented itself of life without *her*. Propped in his strong grasp, she soon recovered, and he told her as much, in a few frank, simple words.

"And yet it must come at last," said she, gently. "What is the short span of a man's life, Esca, for such love as ours? Even had we everything we can wish, all the world can give, there would be a sting in each moment of happiness at the thought that it must end so soon."

"Happiness!" repeated Esca. "What is it? Why is there so little of it on earth? *My* happiness is to be with you, and see, I win it but for an hour at a time, at a cost to yourself I cannot bear to think of."

She looked lovingly in his face. "Do you suppose *I* would count the cost?" said she. "Ever since the night you took me from those fearful revellers, and brought me so gently and so courteously to my father's house, I—I have never forgotten what I owe you."

He raised her hand to his lips, with the action of an inferior doing homage. Alone with the woman he loved, the very depth and generosity of his young affection made him look on her as something sacred and apart.

She hesitated, for she had yet more to say, which maiden shame repressed, lest it should disclose her feelings too openly; but she loved him well, she could not keep silence on so vital a subject, and after a pause, she took courage and asked—

"Esca, could you bear to think we were never to meet again?"

"I would rather die at once!" he exclaimed, fervently.

She shook her head, and smiled rather sadly.

"But *after* death," she insisted, "after death do you believe that you will see me no more?"

He looked blank and confused. The same question had been present almost unconsciously in his mind, but had never taken so definite a shape before.

"You would make me a coward, Mariamne," said he; "when I think of you, I almost *fear* to die."

They were standing under the holm-oak, where the moonlight streamed down clear and cold through the bare branches. It shone on a slab of marble, half-defaced, half-overgrown with moss. Nevertheless, on that surface was distinctly carved the horse's head with which the Roman loved to decorate the stone that marked his last resting-place.

"Do you know what that means?" said she, pointing to this quaint and yet suggestive symbol. "Even the proud Roman feels that death and departure are the same,—that he is going on a journey he knows not where, but one from which he never shall return. It is a journey we must all take, none can tell how soon; for you and me the horse may be harnessed this very night. But

I know where I am going, Esca. If you had slain me an hour ago with your sword, I should have been there even now."

"And I?" he exclaimed. "Should I have been with you? for I would have died amongst the gladiators as I have seen a wolf die in my own country overmatched by hounds. Mariamne, you would not have left me for ever? What would have become of me?"

Again she shook her head with the same pitiful, plaintive smile.

"You do not know the way," said she. "You have no guide to take you by the hand; you would be lost in the darkness; and I,—I should see you no more. Oh! Esca, I can teach you, I can show it you. Let us travel it together, and come what may, we need never part again!"

Then the girl knelt down under that dead tree, with the moonbeams shining on her pale face, and her lips moved in whispered thanksgiving for the late escape, and prayer for him who now stood by her side, and who watched her with wistful looks, as a child watches a piece of mechanism of which he sees plainly the effect, while he strives in vain to comprehend the cause.

It seemed to Esca that the woman he loved

must have found the talisman that all his youth he had felt a vague consciousness he wanted—something beyond manly courage, or burning patriotism, or the dogged obstinacy that fortifies itself by defying the worst. Moreover, the course of his past life, above all, the trials he had lately undergone, could not but have prepared the ground for the reception of that good seed which brings forth such good fruit,—could not but have shown him the necessity for a strength superior to the bravest endurance of mere humanity, for a hope that was fixed beyond the grave. A few minutes she remained on her knees, praying fervently for herself,—for him. He felt that it was so, and while his eyes were riveted on the dear face, so pure and peaceful, turned upward to the sky, he knew that his own being was elevated by her holy influence, that the earthly affection of a lover for his mistress, was in his breast refined by the adoration of a worshipper for a saint.

Then she rose, and taking him by the arm, walked leisurely on her way, discoursing, as she went, on certain truths which she had learnt from Calchas, and which she believed with the faith of those who have been taught by one, himself an eye-witness of the wonders he relates.

There were no dogmas in those early days of the Christian Church to distract the minds of its votaries from the simple tenets of their creed. The grain of mustard-seed had not yet shot up into that goodly tree which has since borne so many branches, and the pruning-knife, hereafter to lop away so many redundant heresies, was not as yet unsheathed. The Christian of the first century held to a very simple exposition of his faith as handed down to him from his Divine Master. Trust and Love were the fundamental rules of his order. Trust, that in the extremity of mortal agony could penetrate beyond the gates of death, and brighten the martyr's face with a ray of splendour, "like the face of an angel." Love, that embraced all things, downward from the Creator to the lowest of the created, that opened its heart freely and ungrudgingly to each, the sinner, the prodigal, and the traveller who fell among thieves. Other faiths, indeed, and other motives have fortified men to march proudly to the stake, to bear without wincing, tortures that forced the sickening spectator to turn shuddering away. A heathen or a Jew could front the lion's sullen scowl, or the grin and glare of the cruel tiger, in the amphitheatre, with the dignified composure that brave men borrow from despair; could behold unmoved the straight cut furrow in the sand that marked the arena of his sufferings, soon to run crimson with his blood. Even athwart the dun smoke, amidst the leaping yellow flames, pale faces have been seen to move, majestic and serene as spectres, with no sustaining power beyond that of a lofty courage, the offspring of education and of pride. But it was the Christian alone who could submit to the vilest degradations and the fiercest sufferings with a humble and even cheerful thankfulness; who could drink from the bitter cup and accept the draught without a murmur, save of regret for his own unworthiness, nay, who could forgive and bless the very tyranny that extorted, the very hand that ministered to, the tortures he endured.

In its early days, fresh from the fountain-head, the Christian's was, indeed, essentially and emphatically a religion of love. To feed the hungry, to clothe the naked, to stretch a hand to the fallen, to think no evil, to judge not, nor to condemn, in short, to love "the brother whom he *had* seen," were the direct commands of that Great Example who had so recently been here on earth. His first disciples strove, hard as fallible humanity can, to imitate him, and in so striving, failed not to attain a certain peaceful composure and contentment of mind, that no other code of morality, no other system of philosophy, had ever yet produced. Perhaps this was the quality that in his dealings with his victim, the Roman executioner found most mysterious and inexplicable. Fortitude, resolution, defiance, these he could understand, but the childlike simplicity that accepted good and evil with equal confidence, that was thankful and cheerful under both, and that entertained neither care for to-day nor anxiety for to-morrow, was a moral elevation, at which, with all their pretensions, his own countrymen had never yet been able to arrive. Neither Stoic nor Epicurean, Sophist nor Philosopher, could look upon life, and death also, with the calm assurance of these unlearned men, leaning on a hand the Roman could not see, convinced of an immortality the Roman was unable to conceive.

With this happy conviction beaming in her face, Mariamne inculcated on Esca the tenets of her noble faith, explaining, not logically indeed but with woman's persuasive reasonings of the heart, how fair was the prospect thus open to him, how glorious the reward, which, though mortal eye could not behold it, mortal hand could not take away. Promises of future happiness are none the less glowing, that they fall on a man's ear from the lips he loves. Conviction goes the straighter to his heart when it pervades another's that beats in unison with his own. Under that moonlit sky, reddened in the horizon with the glare of a distant quarter of the city already set on fire by the insurgents; in that dreary waste of the Esquiline, with its blasted trees, its shrieking night-birds, and its scattered grave-stones, the Briton imbibed the first principles of Christianity from the daughter of Judah, whom he loved; and the girl's face beamed with a holy tenderness more than mortal, while she showed the way of everlasting happiness, and life, and light, to him whose soul was dearer to her than her own.

And meanwhile around them on all sides, murders, rapine, and violence were stalking abroad unchecked. Riotous parties of Vespasian's supporters met, here and there, detached companies of Cæsar's broken legions; and when such collisions took place, the combatants fought madly, as it would seem from mere wanton love of bloodshed, to the death; whichever conquered, neither spared the dissolute citizens, who indeed when safe out of reach, from roofs or windows encouraged the strife heartily with word and gesture. Sparks fell in showers through the streets of Rome, and blood and wine ran in streams along the pavement, nor were the deserted gardens of the Esquiline undisturbed by the tumult and devastation that pervaded the rest of the unhappy city.

CHAPTER XIV.

THE CHURCH.

WHEN they sought to leave their place of refuge Esca and Mariamne found themselves hemmed in and drawn back by the continued tumult that was raging through the surrounding quarters. On all sides were heard the shouts of victory, the shrieks of despair, and the mad riot of drunken mirth. Occasionally flying parties of pursuers or pursued swept through the very outskirts of the gardens themselves, compelling the Briton and his charge to plunge deeper into its gloomy solitudes for concealment.

At length they reached a place of comparative safety, under a knot of dark cypresses that had escaped the general conflagration, and here they paused to take breath and listen, Mariamne becoming every moment more composed and tranquil, while Esca, with a beating heart, calculated the many chances that must still be risked ere they could reach her home beyond the Tiber, and he could place the daughter in safety under her father's roof once more. It was very dark where they were, for the cypresses grew thick and black between them and the sky. The place had probably in former times been a favourite resort in the noonday heat. There were the remains of a grotto or summer-house not yet wholly destroyed, and the fragments of a wide stone basin, from which a fountain had once shot its sparkling drops into the summer air. Several alleys, too, cut in the young plantations, had apparently converged at this spot; and although these were much overgrown and neglected, one still formed, so to speak, a broad, white street of turf, hemmed in by walls of quivering foliage, dark and massive, but sprinkled here and there with points of silver in the moonlight.

Mariamne crept closer to her companion's side.

"I feel so safe and so happy with you," said she, caressingly. "We seem to have changed places. You are the one who is now anxious and—no—not frightened—but ill at ease. Esca! what is it?" she asked with a start, as, looking fondly up in his face, she caught its expression of actual terror and dismay.

His blue eyes were fixed like stone. With parted lips and rigid features, his whole being seemed concentrated into the one effort of seeing, and, backed by the dark shadows of the cypress, his face, usually so frank and fearless, was paler even than her own.

Following with her eyes the direction of his glance, she, too, was something more than startled at what she saw.

Two black figures, clad in long and trailing garments, moved slowly into sight, and crossed the sheet of moonlight which flooded the wide avenue, with solemn step and slow. These again were followed by two in white, looking none the less ghostly that their outlines were so indistinctly defined, the head and feet being alone visible, and the rest of the figure wrapped, as it were, in mist. Then came two more in black, and thus in alternate pairs the unearthly procession glided by; only, ere the half of it had passed, a something, not unlike the human form, draped in a white robe, seemed to float horizontally, at a cubit's height, above the line. A low and wailing chant, too, rose and fell fitfully on the listeners' ears. It was the "Kyrie Eleison," the humble, plaintive dirge in which the Christian mourned, not without hope, for his dead.

Fear was no familiar sentiment in Esca's breast. It could not remain there long. He drew himself up, and the colour rushed back redly to his brow.

"They are spirits!" said he; "spirits of the wood, on whose domains we have trespassed. Good or evil, we will resist them to the last. They will sacrifice us to their vengeance if we show the least signs of fear."

She was proud of his courage even then—the courage that could defy, though it had not been able to shake off, the superstitions of his northern birthplace. It was sweet, too, to think that from her lips he must learn what was truth, both of this world and of the next.

"They are no spirits!" she answered. "They are Christians burying their dead. Esca, we shall be safe with them, and they will show us how to leave this place unobserved."

"Christians?" he replied, doubtfully; "and we, too, are Christians, are we not? I would they were armed, though," he added, reflectively. "With twenty good swordsmen, I would engage to take you unmolested from one end of Rome to the other; but these, I fear, are only priests. Priests! and the legions are loose even now all over the city!"

He was but a young disciple, thought his loving teacher, and many a defeat must be experienced, many a rebuff sustained, ere dependence on his own courage is rooted out of a brave man's heart, to be replaced by that nobler fortitude which relies solely on the will of heaven. Yet a brave man is no bad material out of which to form a good one.

They left their hiding-place, and hastened down the alley after the departing Christians. In a secluded place, where the remaining trees grew thickest and most luxuriant—where the noontide ray had least power to penetrate, the procession had halted. The grave was already being dug. As spadeful after spadeful of loose earth fell with a dull, grating sound on the sward, or trickled back into the cavity, the dirge wailed on, now lowered and repressed like the stifled sob of one who weeps in secret, now rising into notes of chastened triumph, that were almost akin to joy. And here, where Mæcenas, and his poets and his parasites, had met, with garland and goblet, to wile away the summer's day in frivolous disputations, arguing on the endless topics of here and hereafter, life and death, body and soul; groping blindly and in vain throughout the labyrinth for a clue—sneering at Pythagoras, refuting Plato, and maligning Socrates—the body of the dead Christian was laid humbly and trustfully in the earth, and already the departed spirit had learned the efficacy of those truths it had imbibed through scorn and suffering in its lifetime—truths that the heathen sages would have given goblets and garlands, and riches and empire, and all the world besides, but to know and believe in that supreme moment, when all around the dying fades and fails as though it had never been, and there is but one reality from which is no escape.

The Jewess and her champion waited a few paces off while the spade threw its last handfuls to the surface. Then the Christians gathered solemnly and silently round the open grave, and the corpse was lowered gently into its resting-place, and the faces that watched it sink, and stop, and waver, and sink again out of sight, even like the life of the departed, beamed with a holy triumph, for they knew that with this wayfarer, at least, the journey was over and the home attained. Two mourners, somewhat conspicuous from the rest, stood at either end of the grave. The one was a woman, still in the meridian of her beauty; the other a strong, warlike man, scarcely of middle age. The woman's face was turned to heaven, rapt, as it seemed, in an ecstasy of prayer. She was not thinking of the poor remains—the empty shell, consigned beneath her feet to its kindred dust; but with the eye of faith she watched the spirit in its upward flight, and for her the heavens were opened, and her child was even now disappearing through the golden gate. But on the man's contracted features might be read the pain of him who is too weak to bear, and yet too strong to weep. His eye followed with sad, wistful glances clod after clod, as they fell in to cover up the loved and lost. When the earth was flattened down above her head, and not till then, he seemed to look inquiringly at the vacant space amongst the bystanders, and to know that she was gone. He clenched his strong hands tight, and raised his eyes at last. "It is hard to bear," he muttered. "It is very hard to say, 'Thy will be done.'" Then he thought of the empty place at home, and hid his face and wept.

A young girl, on the verge of womanhood, had been called away—called suddenly away—the pride, and the flower, and the darling of her father's house. He was a good man and a brave, and a believer, yet every time his child's face rose up before him, with its bright hair and its loving eyes, something smote him, sharp and cold, like the thrust of a knife.

When the grave was finally closed, the Christians gathered round it in prayer. Mariamne, taking Esca by the hand, came silently among them, and joined in their devotions. It was a strange and solemn sight to the barbarian. A circle of cloaked figures kneeling round an empty space, to worship an unseen power. On either hand a wilderness of ruin and devastation in the heart of a great city; above, an angry glare on the midnight sky, and the shouts of maddened combatants rising and falling on the breeze. By his side, the woman he loved so dearly, and whom he had thought he should never look on again. He knelt with the others, to offer his tribute from a grateful heart. Their prayers were short and fervent, nor did they omit the form their Master had given them expressly for their use. When they rose to their feet, one figure stood forth amongst the rest, and signed for silence with uplifted hand.

This man was obviously a Roman by birth, and spoke his language with the ease, but at the same time with the accent and phrases of the lowest plebeian class. He seemed a handicraftsman by trade, and his palm, when he raised it impressively to bespeak attention, was hardened and scarred with toil. Low of stature, mean in appearance, coarsely clothed, with bare head and feet, there was little in his exterior to command interest or respect, but his frame, square and strongly built, seemed capable of sustaining a vast amount of toil or hardship, while his face, notwithstanding its plain features, denoted repressed enthusiasm, earnest purpose, and honest singleness of heart. He was indeed one of the pioneers of a religion, destined hereafter to cover the surface of the earth. Such were the men who went forth in their Master's name, without scrip, or sandals, or change of raiment, to overrun and conquer the world—who took no thought what they should say when brought before the kings, and governors, and great ones of the earth, trusting only in the sanctity of their mission, and the inspiration under which they spoke. Having little learning, they could refute the wisest philosophers. Having neither rank nor lineage, they could beard the Proconsul on his judgment-seat, or the Cæsar on his throne. Homely and ignorant, they feared not to wander far and wide through strange countries, and hostile nations, spreading the good tidings with a simple ungrudging faith that forced men to believe. Weak by nature it may be, and timid by education, they descended into the arena to meet their martyrdom from the hungry lion, with a quiet fortitude such as neither soldier nor gladiator had courage to display. It was a moral their Master never ceased to inculcate, that his was a message sent not to the noble, and the prosperous, and the distinguished, for these, if they wished to find him, might make their own opportunities to seek him out, but to the poor and lowly, the humble and forlorn, especially to those who were in distress and sorrow, who, having none to help them here, might rely all the more implicitly on his protection, who is emphatically the friend of the friendless.

Therefore, the men who did his work seem to have been chosen principally from the humbler classes of society, from such as could speak to the multitude in homely phrases and with familiar imagery, whose authority the most careless and unthinking might perceive originated in no aid of extraneous circumstances, but came directly from above.

As the speaker warmed to his subject, Esca could not but observe the change that came over the bearing and appearance of his outward man. At first the eye was dull, the speech hesitating, the manner diffident. Gradually a light seemed to steal over his whole countenance, his form towered erect as though it had actually increased in stature, his words flowed freely in a torrent of glowing and appropriate language, his action became dignified, and the whole man clothed himself, as it were, in the majesty of the subject on which he spoke.

That subject was indeed simple enough, sad, it may be, from an earthly point of view, and yet how comforting to the mourners gathered round him beside the new-made grave! At first he contented himself with a short and earnest tribute, clothed in the plainest form of speech, to the worth and endearing qualities of that young girl whom they had just laid in the earth. "She was precious to us all," said he, "yet words like these seem but a mockery to some present here, for whom she was the hope and the joy, and the very light of an earthly home. Grieve, I say, and weep, and wring your hands, for such is man's weak nature, and He who took our nature upon him, sympathizes with our sorrows, and like the good physician, pities while he heals. To-day, your wounds are fresh, your hearts are full, your eyes are blind with tears, you cannot see the truth. To-morrow you will wonder why you mourned so bitterly. To-morrow you will say, 'It is well; we are labouring in the sun, she is resting in the shade; we are hungry and thirsty in a barren land, she is eating the bread and drinking the waters of life, in the garden of Paradise; we are weary and foot-sore, wayfarers still upon the road, but she has reached her home.'

"Yea, now at this very hour, standing here where the earth has just closed over the young face, tender and delicate even in death, would you have her back to you if you could? Those who have considered but the troubles that surround us now, and to whom there is no hereafter, who call themselves philosophers, and whose wisdom is as the wisdom of a blind man walking on the brink of a precipice, have themselves said 'whom the gods love die young;' and will you grudge that your beloved one should have been called out of the vineyard to take her wages, and go to her rest before the burden and heat of the day? Think what her end might have been. Think that you might have offered her up to bear witness to the truth, tied to a stake in the foul arena, face to face with the crouching wild beast gathered for his spring. Ay! and worse even than this might have befallen the child, whom you remember, as it were but yesterday, nestling to her mother's bosom, or clinging round her father's knees! 'The Christians to the Panther, and the maidens to the Pandar!'* You have heard the brutal shouts and shuddered with fear and anger while you heard. And you would have offered her, as Abraham offered Isaac, beating your breasts, and holding your breath for very agony the while. But is it not better thus? She has earned the day's wages, labouring but for an hour at sunrise; she has escaped the cross, and yet has won the crown!

"But you who hear me, envy not this young maiden, though she be now arrived where all so long to go. Rather be proud and happy, that

* "Christiani ad leones! Virgines ad lenones!"—a sentence that found no small favour with the Roman crowd.

your Master cannot spare you, that he has yet work for you to do. To every man's hand is set his appointed task, and every man shall find strength given him to fulfil it when the time arrives. Some of you will bear witness before Cæsar, and for such the scourges are already knotted and the cross is reared; but to these I need scarcely speak of loyalty, for to them the very suffering brings with it its own fortitude, and they are indeed blessed who are esteemed worthy of the glory of martyrdom! Some must go forth to preach the gospel in wild and distant lands; and well I know that neither toil, nor hardship, nor peril, will cause them to waver an hair's-breadth from their path, yet have they difficulties to meet, and foes to contend with, that they know not of. Let them beware of pride and self-sufficiency, lest in raising the altar, they make the sacrifice of more account than the spirit in which it is offered—lest in building the church they take note of every stone in the edifice, and lose sight of the purpose for which it was reared. But ye cannot all be martyrs, nor preachers, nor prophets nor chief-priests, yet every one of you, even the weakest and the lowest here present—woman, child, slave, or barbarian—is none the less a soldier and a servant of the cross! Every one has his duty to do, his watch to keep, his enemy to conquer. It is not much that is required of you, little indeed in comparison with all you have received—but that little must be given without reserve, and with the whole heart. Has any one of you left a duty unfulfilled? when he departs from hence let him go home and accomplish it. Has any one an enemy? let him be reconciled. Has he done his brother a wrong? let him make amends. Has he sustained an injury? let him forgive it. Even as you have laid in the grave the perishable body of the departed, so lay down here every unearthly weakness, every unholy wish, and every evil thought. Nay, as these Chief Mourners have to-night parted and weaned themselves from that which they loved best on earth, so must you tear out and cast away from you the truest and dearest affections that stand between you and your service, ay, even though you rend them from the very inner chambers of your heart. And then with constant effort, and never-ceasing prayer, striving, step by step, and winning, inch by inch, now slipping back it may be where the path is treacherous, and the hill is steep, to rise from your knees, humbled and therefore stronger, gaining more than you have lost, you shall arrive at last, where there is no strife, and no failing, where she for whom you weep to-night is even now in glory, where He whom you follow has already prepared a place for you, and where you who have loved and trusted, shall be happy for evermore!"

Ceasing, he spread his hands abroad, and implored a blessing on those who heard him, after which the Christians breaking up their circle, gathered round the bereaved parents, with a few quiet words and gestures of sympathy, such as those offer who have themselves experienced the sorrows they are fain to assuage.

"I am in safety here," whispered Mariamne to the Briton, as she pointed out a dark figure, with white flowing locks, whom he now recognized as Calchas. In another moment she was in the old man's arms, who raised his eyes to heaven, and thanked God with heartfelt gratitude for her deliverance.

"Your father and I," said he, "have sought you with fearful anxiety, and even now he is raising some of his countrymen to storm the Tribune's house, and take you from it with the strong hand. Mariamne, you hardly know how much your father loves his child. And I too was disturbed for your safety, but I trusted—trusted in that heaven which never fails the innocent. Nevertheless, I sought for aid among my brethren and they have raised, even the poorest of them, such a sum as would have tempted the Prætor to interfere, even against a man like Placidus. I did but remain with them to say a prayer while they buried their dead. But now you are safe, and you will come back with me to your father's house, and one of these whom I can trust shall go to tell him at the place where his friends were to assemble; and Esca, thy preserver for the second time, who is to me as a son, shall accompany us home—though we shall not need a guard, for thy father's friends, tried warriors every man, and armed, will meet us ere we leave the wilderness for the streets."

It was a strong temptation to the Briton, but the words he had so lately heard had sunk deep into his heart. He, too, would fain cast in his lot amongst these earnest men. He, too, he thought, had a task to perform—a cherished happiness to forego. With a timely warning, it might be in his power to save the Emperor's life, and his very eagerness to accompany Mariamne but impressed him the more with the conviction that it was his duty to leave her, now she was in comparative safety, and hasten on his errand of mercy. Calchas, too, insisted strongly on this view, and though Mariamne was silent, and even pleaded with her eyes against the risk, he turned stoutly from their influence, and ere she was clasped in her father's arms, the new Christian was already half-way between the Esquiline and the palace of Cæsar.

CHAPTER XV.

REDIVIVUS.

MANY had been the debauch at which, himself its chief originator and promoter, the Tribune had assisted; nor had he escaped the penalties that Nature exacts even from the healthiest constitutions, when her laws are habitually outraged in the high-tide of revelry and mirth; but never, after his longest sittings with the Emperor, had he experienced anything to compare with the utter prostration of mind and body in which he came to himself, waking from the death-like sleep that followed his pledge to Valeria. With returning consciousness came a sense of painful giddiness, which, as the velvet cushions of the couch rose and heaved beneath his sight, confused him utterly as to where he was, or how he got there; then, sitting up with an effort that seemed to roll a ball of lead across his brain, he was aware that every vein throbbed at fever-heat, that his hands were numbed and swollen, that his mouth was parched, his lips cracked, and that he had a racking headache—the latter symptom was sufficiently familiar to be reassuring; he sprang to his feet, regardless of the pang so sudden a movement shot through his frame, then seizing a goblet from the table, filled it to the brim with Falernian, and in defiance of the nausea with which its very fragrance overpowered him, emptied it to the dregs. The effect, as he expected, was instantaneous; it enabled him to stand erect, and, passing his hand across his brow, by a strong effort of the will, he forced himself to connect and comprehend the events that had led to this horrible and bewildering trance. By degrees, one after another, like links in a chain, he traced the doings of the day, and beginning a long way back, somewhere about noon, till the immediate past, so to speak, came more and more tangibly within his grasp. It was with a thrill of triumphant pleasure, that he remembered Valeria's visit, and his own arm winding round her handsome form on that very couch. Where was she now? He looked about him vacantly, almost expecting to find her in the room; as he did so, his eye lighted on the two goblets, one of them half-emptied, still standing on their salver.

To say that Placidus had a conscience would be simply a perversion of terms; for that monitor, never very troublesome, had since his manhood been so stifled and silenced as to have become a mere negative quality, yet in his present unhinged state, a shudder of horror did come over him, as he recalled the visit to Petosiris, and the poison with which he had resolved to insure the silence of his slave. But ere that shudder passed away, the dark secret Esca knew, the plot from which it was now too late to draw back, the desperate adventure that every hour brought nearer, and that must be attempted to-night, all these considerations came flooding in on his memory at once, and for a moment he felt paralyzed by the height of the precipice on the brink of which he stood. With the emergency, however, as was always the case in the Tribune's character, came the energy required to encounter it. "At least," he muttered, steadying himself by the table with one hand, "the cup is nearly empty, the drug cannot but have done its work. First, I must make sure of the carrion, and then it will be time enough to find Valeria." Had he suffered less in body, he would have laughed his own low malicious laugh, to think how deftly he had outwitted the woman he professed to love. The laugh, however, died away in a grin that betrayed more of pain than mirth; and the Tribune, with chattering teeth and shaking frame, and wavering uncertain steps, betook himself to the outer court to make sure with his own eyes that the stalwart frame of him whom he feared was stiff and cold in death.

His first feeling would have been one of acute apprehension, had not anger so completely mastered that sensation, when he perceived the slave's chain and collar lying coiled on the pavement. Obviously, Esca had escaped, and was gone, moreover, with his late master's life completely in his power; but Placidus possessed a keen intellect and one familiar with sudden combinations; it flashed upon him at once, that he had been outwitted by Valeria, and the two had fled together.

The sting was very sharp, but it roused and sobered him. Pacing swiftly back through the corridors, and stopping for a few minutes to immerse his head and face in cold water, he returned to the banqueting-hall, and eagerly scrutinized with look and smell, and, notwithstanding all that had happened, even with a sparing taste, the cup from which he had last drunk. The opiate, however, had been so skilfully prepared that nothing suspicious could be detected in the flavour of the wine; nevertheless, reflecting on all the circumstances with a clearer head, as the strength of his constitution gradually asserted itself, he arrived at the true conclusion, and was satisfied that Valeria had changed the cups while his attention was distracted by her charms; that he had purchased a poison he never doubted for a moment, nor suspected that Petosiris could have dared, from sheer love of trickery, to substitute an opiate for the deadlier draught; but he exulted to think that his powerful organization must have resisted its effects, and that he who had so often narrowly escaped death in the field must indeed bear a charmed life. If a suspicion haunted him that the venom might still be lurking in his system, to do its work more completely after a short respite, the vague horror of such a thought did but goad him to make use of the intervening time all the more ardently for business and pleasure, not forgetting the sacred duty of revenge. "*Dum vivimus vivamus,*" was the Tribune's motto, and if he had been granted but one hour to live, he would have divided that hour systematically, between the delights of love, wine, and mischief.

Rapidly, though coolly, he reviewed his position, as though he had been commanding a cohort hemmed in by the Jewish army. To-night would make or mar him. The gladiators would be here within an hour. Esca must, ere this, have reached the palace and given the alarm. Why had a centurion of Cæsar not yet arrived with a sufficient guard to arrest him in his own house? They might be expected at any moment. Should he fly while there was yet time? What! and lose the brilliant future so nearly within his reach? No—he would weather this, as he had weathered other storms, by skilful and judicious steering. A man who has no scruples need never be deficient in resource. To leave his house now, would be a tacit admission of guilt. To be found alone, undefended, unsuspicious, a strong presumption of innocence. He would at least have sufficient interest to be taken into the presence of Cæsar. There, what so easy as to accuse the slave of treachery, to persuade the Emperor the barbarian had but hatched a plot against his master's life; to make the good-humoured old glutton laugh with an account of the drugged goblet, and finish the night by a debauch with his imperial host?

Then, he must be guided by the preparations for defence which he observed in the palace. If they were weak, he must find some means of communicating with Hippias, and the attack would be facilitated by his own presence inside. If, on the contrary, there was an obvious intention of firm resistance, the conspirators must be warned to postpone their enterprise. If worst came to the worst, he could always save his own head by informing against his confederates and so handing over Hippias and the gladiators to death.

Some slight compunction visited him at the thought of such an alternative, but he soon stifled it with the arguments of his characteristic philosophy. Should he be found, indeed, presiding at a supper-party composed of these desperate men, they might defend the gate whilst he fled directly to Cæsar, and sacrificed them at once. Under any circumstances, he argued, he had bought them, and had a right to make use of them.

In the meantime, Mariamne would be here directly. She ought to have been here long ago. Whatever the future threatened, an hour, half an hour, a quarter, should be devoted to her society, and after that, come what might, at least he would not have been foiled in every event of the day. It was when he had arrived at this conclusion, that Esca from his hiding-place saw the figure of the Tribune, pale, wan, and ghostly, giving directions for the preparation of the supper-table.

The evening stole on, the sun-dial no longer showed the hour, and the slave whose duty it was to keep count of time by the water-clock * then in vogue, announced that the first watch of the night was already advanced. He was followed by Automedon, who came into the presence of his master, with hanging head and sheepish looks, sadly mistrusting how far his own favour would

* The *clepsydra*, or water-clock—a Greek invention for the division of time—consisting of a hollow globe made of glass, or some transparent substance, from which the water trickled out through a narrow orifice, in quantities so regulated, that the sinking level of the element marked with sufficient exactitude the time that had elapsed since the vessel was filled.

bear him harmless in the delivery of the tidings he had to impart. It was always a perilous duty to inform Placidus of the failure of any of his schemes. He listened, indeed, with a calm demeanour and an unmoved countenance, but sooner or later he surely contrived to visit on the unfortunate messenger, the annoyance he himself experienced from the message.

The Tribune's face brightened as the boy came into the hall; with characteristic duplicity, however, he veiled even from his charioteer the impatience in which he had waited his return.

"Have you brought the horses in cool?" said he, with an affectation of extreme indifference.

Automedon looked greatly relieved.

"Quite cool," he answered, "most Illustrious! and Oarses came part of the way home, but he got down near the Sacred Gate, and I had no one with me in the chariot the whole length of the Flaminian Way; and the slaves will be back presently; and Damasippus.—Oh! my lord, do not be angry!—Damasippus—I fear I have left him dead in the street."

Here the lad's courage failed him completely; he had indeed been thoroughly frightened by the events of the night; and making a piteous face, he twined his fingers in his long curls, and wept aloud.

"What! fool!" thundered the Tribune, his brow turning black with rage. "You have not brought her after all! Silly child," he added, controlling himself with a strong effort. "Where is the—the passenger—I charged Damasippus to bring here with him to-night?"

"I will tell you the truth," exclaimed the boy, flinging himself down on his knees, and snatching at the hem of his master's garment. "By the Temple of Vesta I will tell you the truth. I drove from here across Tiber, and I waited in the shadow by Tiber-side; and Jugurtha wouldn't stand still, and presently Damasippus brought a—a passenger, in his arms, and put it into the chariot, and bade me go on fast; and we went on at a gallop till we tried to cross the Appian Way, and then we had to turn aside, for the houses were burning and the people fighting in the street, and Scipio was frightened and pulled, and Jugurtha wouldn't face the crowd, and I drove on to cross a little farther down, but we were stopped again by the Vestals, and I couldn't drive through them! So we halted to let them pass, and then, a fierce terrible giant caught the horses and stopped them once more, and a thousand soldiers, nay, a legion at least, surrounded the chariot, and they killed Damasippus, and they tore the passenger out, and killed it too, and Scipio kicked, and I was frightened, and drove home as fast as I could—and indeed it wasn't my fault!"

Automedon's fears had magnified both the number of the assailants and the dangers undergone. He had not recognised the gladiators, and was altogether in too confused a state, as the Tribune perceived at a glance, to afford his master any more coherent information than the foregoing. Placidus bit his lip in baffled anger, for he could not see his way; nevertheless the boy-charioteer was a favourite, and he would not visit the failure of the enterprise on him.

"I am glad the horses are safe," said he, good-humouredly. "Go, get some supper and a cup of wine. I will send for you again presently."

Automedon, agreeably surprised, glanced up at his master's face ere he departed, and observed that, although deadly pale, it had assumed the fixed resolute expression his dependents knew so well.

He had indeed occasion to summon all the presence of mind on which he prided himself, for even while he spoke, his quick ear caught the tramp of feet, and the familiar clink of steel. The blood gathered round his heart as he contemplated the possibility that a maniple of Cæsar's guards might even now be occupying the court. It was with a sigh of intense relief, that instead of the centurion's eagle-crest, he recognized the tall form of Rufus, accompanied by his comrades, advancing respectfully, and even with awkward diffidence, through the outer hall.

The Tribune could assume—none better—any character it suited him to play at a moment's notice; nevertheless there was a ring of real cordiality in his greeting, for the visitors were more welcome than they guessed.

"Hail! Rufus, Lutorius, Eumolpus!" he shouted boisterously. "Gallant swordsmen, and deep drinkers all! What! old Hirpinus, do I not see thy broad shoulders yonder in the rear? and Hippias too, the king of the arena! Welcome, every man of you! Even now the feast is spread, and the Chian cooling yonder amongst the flowers. Once again, a hearty welcome to you all!"

The gladiators, still somewhat abashed by the unaccustomed splendour which met their eyes on every side, responded with less than their usual confidence to their entertainer. Rufus nudged

Lutorius to reply in polite language, and the Gaul in a fit of unusual modesty, passed the signal on to Eumolpus of Ravenna—a beetle-browed bow-legged warrior, with huge muscles and a heavy sullen face. This champion looked helplessly about him and seemed inclined to turn tail and fly, when to his great relief, Hippias advanced from the rear of his comrades, and created a diversion in his favour, of which he availed himself by slinking incontinently into the background.

Placidus clapped his hands, an Asiatic fashion affected by the more luxurious Romans; and two or three slaves appeared in obedience to the summons. The gladiators looked on in awe at the sumptuous dresses and personal beauty of these domestics.

"Hand round wine here amongst my friends: I will but say three words to your captain, and we will go to supper forthwith."

So speaking, the Tribune led Hippias apart, having resolved that in the present critical state of affairs, it would be better to take him entirely into his confidence, and trust to the scrupulous notions of fidelity to their bargains, which such men entertained, for the result.

"There is no time to lose," observed he anxiously, when he had led Hippias apart from his followers. "Something has occurred which was out of all our calculations. Can they overhear us, think ye?"

The fencing-master glanced carelessly at his band. "Whilst they are at *that* game," said he, "they would not hear the assembly sounding from all four quarters of the camp. Never fear, Illustrious! it will keep them busy till supper-time."

The band had broken up into pairs, and were hard at work with their favourite pastime, old as the Alban hills, and handed down to the Roman empire from the dynasty of the Pharaohs. It consisted in gambling for small coins at the following trial of skill:

The players sat or stood, face to face; each held the left hand erect, on which he marked the progress of his game. With the right he shot out any one or more of his four fingers and thumb, or all together, with immense rapidity, guessing aloud at the same time the sum total of the fingers thus brandished by himself and his adversary, who was employed in the same manner. Whoever guessed right won a point, which was immediately marked on the left, held immoveable at shoulder-height for the purpose, and when five of these had been won, the game began again. Nothing could be more simple, nothing apparently less interesting, and yet it seemed to engross the attention of the gladiators to the exclusion of all other subjects, even the prospect of supper and the flavour of the Falernian.*

"They are children now," said Placidus, contemptuously. "They will be men presently, and tigers to-night. Hippias, the slave has escaped. We must attack the palace forthwith."

"I know it," replied the other quietly. "But the Germans are relieving guard at this hour. My own people are hardly ready, and it is not dark enough yet."

"You know it!" repeated Placidus, even more irritated than astonished by his companion's coolness, "you *know* it, and yet you have not hastened your preparations! Do you know, too, that this yellow-haired barbarian has got your head, and mine, and all the empty skulls of our intelligent friends who are amusing themselves yonder, under

* This game is played to-day with equal zest, under its Italian name of "Morro." Perhaps its nature was best rendered by the Latin phrase "micare digites," "to flash the fingers."

his belt? Do you know that Cæsar, true to his swinish propensities, will turn like a hunted boar, when he suspects the least shadow of danger? Do you know that not one of us may live to eat the very supper waiting for us in the next room? What are you made of, man, that you can thus look me so coolly in the face with the sword at both our throats?"

"I can keep my own throat with my hand," replied the other, totally unmoved by his host's agitation. "And I am certainly not accustomed to fear danger *before* it comes. But that the barbarian had escaped I saw with my own eyes, for I left him ten minutes since within a hundred paces of your own gate."

The Tribune's eyebrows went up in unfeigned surprise.

"Then he has not reached the palace!" he exclaimed, speaking rather to himself than his informant.

"Not reached the palace certainly," replied the latter, calmly, "since I tell you I saw him here. And in very good company too," he added, with a smile.

The Tribune's astonishment had for once deprived him of his self-command.

"With Valeria?" he asked, unguardedly; and directly he had spoken a vague suspicion made him wish that he had held his tongue.

The fencing-master started and knit his brows. His head was more erect and his voice sterner when he answered—

"I have seen the Lady Valeria too, within the last hour. She had no slaves with her beyond her usual attendants."

Anger, curiosity, uncertainty, jealousy, a hundred conflicting emotions were rankling at the Tribune's heart. What had this handsome gladiator to do at Valeria's house? and was it possible that she did not care for the slave after all? Then what could have been her object throughout? He marked too the alteration in manner betrayed by Hippias at the mention of this fair and flighty dame; nor did it seem improbable under all the circumstances that he entertained a kindly feeling, if nothing more, for his pupil. Judging men and women by his own evil nature, and knowing well the favour with which their female admirers regarded these votaries of the sword, the Tribune did not hesitate to put its true construction on such kindly feelings, and their probable result.

From that moment he hated Hippias—hated him all the more that in the tumult and confusion of the coming night he might find an opportunity of gratifying his hatred by the destruction of the gladiator. Many a bold leader has been struck down from behind by the very followers he was encouraging; and who would ask how a conspirator met his death, in the attack on a palace, and the murder of an emperor? Even while the thought crossed his mind he took the other by the hand, and laughed frankly in his face.

"Thou art at home in the private apartments of every lady in Rome, I believe, my warlike Apollo," said he. "But, indeed, it is no question now of such trifling; the business of to-night must be determined on—ay, and disposed of—without delay. If my slave had reached the palace our whole plan must have been altered. I wish, as you did come across him, you had treated him to that deadly thrust of yours under the short-ribs, and brought him in here dead or alive."

"He will not trouble us," observed the other, coolly. "Take my word for it, Tribune, he is disposed of for the present."

"What mean you?" asked Placidus, a devilish

joy lighting up his sallow face. "Did you bribe him to secrecy then and there with the metal you are accustomed to lavish so freely? Gold will buy silence for a time, but steel insures it for ever."

"Nay, Tribune," answered Hippias, with a frank laugh. "We have been fencing too long in the dark. I will tell you the whole truth. This young giant of yours is safe enough for the present. I saw him depart with a pale-faced girl, in a black hood, whom he promised to take care of as far as Tiber-side. Depend upon it he will think of nothing else to-night. For all his broad shoulders, the down is yet upon his chin. And a man's beard must be gray before he leaves such a fair young lass as that to knock his head against a wall, even though it be the wall of a palace. No, no, Tribune, he is safe enough, I tell you, for the next twelve hours, at least!"

"A pale-faced girl?" repeated Placidus, still harping on Valeria. "What, and who was she? Did you know her? did you speak to her?"

"My people had some wild tale," replied the fencing-master, "about a chariot with white horses, that had been upset in the street, and a girl all gagged and muffled, whom they pulled out of it, and for whom, of course, they quarrelled amongst themselves. In faith, had it not been for to-night's business and the oath, you might have seen some sweet practice in your own porch, for I have two or three here that can make as close and even work with a sword as a tailor does with his needle. They said something about her being a Jewess. Very likely she may be, for they swarm across Tiber; since we have lost Nero. And the lad might as well be a Jew as a Briton for that matter. Are you satisfied now, Tribune? By the belly of Bacchus, I must wash my mouth out with Falernian. All this talking makes a man as thirsty as a camel."

Satisfied! and after what he had just learnt! Chariot! White horses! Jewess! There could be no doubt of it. These gladiators must have blundered on her, thought the Tribune, and slain my freedman, and rescued her from my people, and handed her over to the man whom most I hate and fear on earth. Satisfied! Perhaps I shall be better satisfied when I have captured her, and humbled Valeria, and put *you* out of the way, my gallant cut-throat, and seen the slave scourged to death at my own door-post! Then, and not till then, shall I be able to drink my wine without a heartburn, and lay my head on the pillow with some chance of sleep. In the meantime, to-night's work must be done. To-night's work, that puts Vespasian virtually on the throne, (for this boy* of his shall only keep the cushion warm till his father takes his seat), that makes Placidus the first man in the empire. Nay, that might even open a path to the Purple itself. The General is well advanced in years; already somewhat broken and worn with his campaigns. Titus indeed, is the darling of the legions, but all the heart black-browed Berenice has left him, is wrapped up in war. He loves it, I verily believe—the daring fool!—for the mere braying of trumpets, and the clash of steel. Not a centurion exposes himself half so freely, nor so often. Well, a Zealot's javelin, or a stone from the ramparts of some nameless town in Judæa, may dispose of him at any time. Then there is but Domitian. A clever youth indeed, and an unscrupulous. So much the worse for him! A mushroom is not the only dish that may be fatal to an emperor, and if the knot be so secure as to baffle all dexterity, why, it must be cut with steel. Ay, the Macedonian knew well how the great game should be played. Satisfied!

* Domitian.

Like him, I shall never be satisfied while there is anything more to win!

These being the Tribune's thoughts, it is needless to say that he assumed a manner of the utmost frankness and carelessness.

"Thirsty!" he repeated, in a loud voice, clapping Hippias on the shoulder. "Thirsty—I could empty an aqueduct! Welcome again, and heartily, my heroes all! See, the supper waits. Let us go in and drink out the old Falernian!"

CHAPTER XVI.

"MORITURI."

KNOWING well with whom he was to deal, Placidus had ordered a repast to be prepared for his guests on a scale of magnificence unusual even in his luxurious dwelling. It was advisable, not only to impose on these rude natures with unaccustomed pomp and parade, but also to excite their cupidity by the display of gold and jewels while their fiercer passions were inflamed with wine. The more reckless and desperate they could be rendered the more fit would they be for his purpose. There were the tools, sharp and ready for use, but he thought they would admit of a yet finer edge, and prepared to put it on accordingly.

Therefore, he had ordered the supper to be laid in an inner apartment, reserved for occasions of especial state, and in which it was whispered that Vitellius himself had more than once partaken of his subject's hospitality; nay, had even expressed gratification with his entertainment. And which, while blazing with as much of ornament and decoration as could be crowded into a supper-room, was of such moderate dimensions as to bring all the costly objects it contained within notice of the guests. The tessellated pavement was of the richest and gaudiest squares, laid together as smooth and bright as glass. The walls were of polished citron-wood, heavily gilded round the skirting and edges, while the panels were covered in the florid and gradually deteriorating taste of the period, with paintings, brilliant in colour, and beautiful in execution. These represented mythological subjects not of the purest nature, but fauns, nymphs, and satyrs were to be found in the majority, while Bacchus himself was more than once repeated in all the glory of his swaying paunch; his garland of vine-leaves, his ivy-covered wand, and surrounding clusters of rich, ripe, purple grapes. To fill the niches between these panels, the goat—an animal always associated in the Roman mind with wine, perhaps because he drinks no water—was imitated in precious metals, and in every attitude. Here they butted, there they browsed, in another corner a pair of them frisked and gambolled in living kid-like glee, while yonder, horned and bearded, a venerable sage in silver gazed upon the guests with a wise Arcadian simplicity that was almost ludicrous. The tables, which were removed with every change of dishes, were of cedar, supported on grotesque claws of bronze, heavily gilt; the couches, framed of ivory and gold, were draped in various coloured shawls of the softest Asiatic texture, and strewed with cushions of so rich a crimson as to border nearly on Imperial purple. No dish was of a meaner metal than gold, and the drinking-cups, in which Falernian blushed, or Chian sparkled, were studded with rubies, emeralds, pearls, and other precious stones. The sharp nail of a gladiator might at any moment have picked out unobserved, that which would have purchased his freedom and his life, but the men were honest, as they understood the term, and the gems were as safe here, and indeed a good deal safer, than they would have been in the temple of Vesta, or of the Capitoline Jove himself. In a recess at one end of the apartment, reared like an altar upon three wide low carpetted steps, from each of which censers exhaled aromatic odours, stood the sideboard of polished walnut, carved in exquisite imitation of birds, insects, reptiles, flowers, and fruit. This was covered by a snowy cloth, and on it glittered, richly chased and burnished, the Tribune's store of golden cups and vases, which men quoted at every supper-table in Rome.

Lutorius reclining opposite this blaze of magnificence, shaded his eyes with his hand.

"What is it, my bold Gaul?" asked his host, raising himself on his elbow to pledge him, and signing to a slave to fill the swordsman's cup. "Hast thou got thy guard up already to save thy face?'

"They dazzle me, most Illustrious!" answered the ready Gaul. "I had rather blink at the sunrise flashing on the blue waters from Ostia. I did not think there had been so much gold in Rome."

"He has not seen the palace yet," said Placidus, laughing, as he emptied his cup and turned to the other guests. "Some of us will indeed be dazzled to-night, if I mistake not. What think ye, my friends, must be the plates and drinking-vessels, where the very shields and helmets of the guards are solid gold? Meantime, let us wash our eyes with Falernian, lest we mistake our way and intrude on the privacy of Cæsar in the dark."

So appropriate a sentiment met with universal approval. The gladiators laughed loudly, and proffered their cups to be filled. There was no question now of secresy or disguise; there was even no further affectation of ignoring the purpose for which they had met, or the probable result of the night's enterprise. Eumolpus, indeed, and one or two more of the thicker-witted, satisfied to know that the present moment brought a magnificent reception, and an abundance of good cheer, were willing to remain in uncertainty about the future, resolving simply to obey the orders of their captain, and to ask no questions; but even these could not help learning by degrees that they had before them no work of ordinary bloodshed; but that they were involved in a conspiracy which was to determine the empire of the world. It did not destroy their appetite, though it may have increased their thirst.

In proportion as the wine flowed faster the guests lost their diffidence and found their tongues. Their host exerted himself to win golden opinions from all, and entered with ready tact into the characteristics and peculiarities of each.

"Eumolpus!" said he, as a slave entered, bearing an enormous turbot on a yet larger dish, "fear not to encounter him. He is a worthy foe, and a countryman of thine own. He left Ravenna but yesterday. In truth, that fair-built town sends us the widest turbots and the broadest shoulders in the empire. Taste him, man, with a cup of Chian, and say if the trainer's rations have spoiled thy palate for native food."

Half-brutalised as he was by nature and education, the gladiator had still a kindly feeling for his birthplace. Even now a memory of his boyhood would sometimes steal across him like a dream. The stretch of sand, the breezy Adriatic, the waves dashing against the harbour-walls, and a vision of curly-headed, black-eyed children, of whom he was one, tumbling and playing on the shore. He felt more human when he thought of such things. While the Tribune spoke he rose in his own esteem, for his host treated him like a man rather than a beast, and those few careless words gained a champion for Placidus, who was ready to follow him to the death.

So was it with the rest. To Rufus he enlarged on the happiness of a country life, and the liberty —none the less dear for being imaginary—enjoyed by a Roman citizen, who, within easy distance of the capital, could sit beneath his own porch to watch the sunset crimsoning the Apennines, and tread into home-made wine the grapes of his own vineyard. He talked of pruning the elms and training the vines, of shearing sheep and goading oxen, as though he had been a rustic all his life, seasoning such glowing descriptions to suit his listener's palate, with the charms even of winter in the snow amongst the hills, the boar driven through the leafless copse, the wild-fowl lured from the half-frozen lake, the snug and homely roof, the crackling fire, and the children playing on the hearth.

"'Tis but another night-watch," said he, cordially, "and it will be my turn to sup with thee in thy mountain-home. Half a dozen such strokes as I have seen thee deal in mere sport, my hero! and thou wilt never need to meddle with steel again, save in the form of a ploughshare or a hunting-spear. By the fillet of Ceres! my friends, there is a golden harvest, to-night, only waiting for the sickle!"

And Rufus, for whom a few acres of Italian soil and liberty to cultivate them in peace, with his wife and children, comprised all of happiness that life could give, contemplated the prospect thus offered with an imagination heated by wine, and a determination, truly formidable in a man of his quiet, dogged resolution, if hard fighting was to count for anything, not to fail in at least deserving his reward.

"Hirpinus!" exclaimed the host, turning to the veteran, who was a sworn lover of good cheer, and had already consumed supper enough for two ordinary men, washed down by proportionate draughts of wine, "thy favourite morsel is even now leaving the spit. Pledge me in Falernian ere it comes. Nay, spoil it not with honey, which I hold to be a mistake unworthy of a gladiator. We will pour a libation to Diana down our throats, in her capacity of huntress only, my friend; I care not for the goddess in any other. Ho! slaves! bring here some wild boars!"

As he spoke the domestics reappeared, in pairs, carrying between them as many wild boars, roasted whole, as there were guests. One of these huge dishes was set aside for each man, and the carvers proceeded to their duty, unmoved by the ejaculations of amazement that broke from the gladiators at such prodigal magnificence.

Their attention was, however, somewhat distracted at this stage of the feast by the entrance of Euchenor, who slunk to the place reserved for him with a shade of sullen disappointment lowering on his brow.

The host, however, had resolved that nothing should occur to mar the success of his entertainment, so refrained from asking any questions as to his absence, and motioned him courteously to a couch, with as frank a greeting as though he had been aware of its cause. He suspected treachery, notwithstanding, none the less that Euchenor hastened to explain his tardy arrival. "He had heard a tumult in the neighbourhood," he said, "whilst the guests were entering the house, and had visited the nearest post of his comrades to ascertain that they had not been attacked. It was some distance to the palace-gardens, and he could not avoid missing the earlier stages of the banquet."

"You must make up for lost time," observed Placidus, signing to the slaves to heap the new comer's plate and fill his cup to the brim. "The later, the warmer welcome; the earlier, the better cheer," and whilst he spoke the friendly words he was resolving that the Greek should be placed in front that whole night, under his immediate supervision. At the slightest symptom of treachery or wavering, he would slay him with his own hand.

And now the gigantic hunger of these champions seemed to be appeased at last. Dish had succeeded dish in endless variety, and they had applied themselves to each as it came with an undiminished energy that astonished the domestics accustomed to the palled appetites of jaded men of pleasure like their lord. Even the latter—though he tried hard, for he especially prided himself on his powers of eating and drinking—found it impossible to keep pace with his guests. Their great bodily powers, indeed, increased by severe and habitual training, enabled them to consume vast quantities of food, without experiencing those sensations of lassitude and repletion which overcome weaker frames. It seemed as though most of what they ate went at once to supply the waste created by years of toil, and as soon as swallowed fed the muscles instead of burdening the stomach. It was equally so with wine. Such men can drink draught after draught, and partake freely in the questionable pleasures of intoxication, whilst they pay none of its penalties. A breath of fresh air, a few minutes' exercise, and their brains are cool, their eyes clear, their whole system strengthened for the time and stimulated, rather than stupefied, by their excess.

The gladiators lay back on their couches in extreme bodily content. The cups were still quickly filled and emptied, but more in compliance with the customs of conviviality than the demands of thirst. They were all talking at once, and every man saw both present and future through the rosy medium of the wine he had imbibed.

There were two, however, of the party who had not suffered their real inmost attention to stray for an instant from the actual business of the night, who calculated the time exactly as it passed, who watched the men through the succeeding phases of satisfaction, good-humour, conviviality, and recklessness, stopping just short of inebriety, and seized the very moment at which the iron was hot enough to strike. The same thought was in the brain of each, when their eyes met; the same words were springing to their lips, but Hippias spoke first.

"No more wine to-night, Tribune, if work is to de done! The circus is full; the arena swept; the show paid for. When the Prætor takes his seat we are ready to begin."

Placidus glanced significantly in his face, and

rose, holding a brimming goblet in his hand. The suddenness of the movement arrested immediate attention. The men were all silent, and looking towards their host.

"Good friends!" said he. "Trusty swordsmen! Welcome guests! Listen to me. To-night we burn the palace—we overthrow the empire—we hurl Cæsar from his throne. All this you know, but there is something more you do not know. One has escaped who is acquainted with the plot. In an hour it may be too late. We are fast friends, we are in the same galley—the land is not a bow-shot off. But the wind is rising—the water rushing in beneath her keel. Will you bend your backs forthwith and row the galley safe home with me?"

The project was a favourite one, the metaphor suited to their tastes. As the Tribune paused, acclamations greeted him on all sides, and "We will! We will!" "Through storm and sunshine!" "Against wind and weather!" sprung from many an eager lip. It was obvious the men were ready for anything, "One libation to Pluto!" added the host, emptying his cup, and the guests leaping to their feet followed his example with a mad cheer. Then they formed in pairs, as they were accustomed in the amphitheatre, and Euchenor with a malicious laugh exclaimed, "Morituri te salutant!"

It was enough! The ominous words were caught up and repeated in wild defiance and derision, boding small scruples of mercy or remorse. Twice they marched round the supper-room to the burden of that ghastly chant, and when shaking off the fumes of wine they snatched eagerly at their arms, Placidus put himself at their head with a triumphant conviction that come what might, they would not fail him in his last desperate throw for the great game.

CHAPTER XVII.

THE GERMAN GUARD.

ALL was in confusion at the palace of the Cæsars. The civil war that had now been raging for several hours in the capital, the tumults that pervaded every quarter of the city, had roused the alarm, and to a certain extent the vigilance of such troops as still owned allegiance to Vitellius. But late events had much slackened the discipline for which Roman soldiers were so famous, and that could be but a spurious loyalty which depended on amount of pay and opportunities for plunder, which was accustomed moreover to see the diadem transferred from one successful general to another at a few months' interval. Perhaps his German guards were the only soldiers of Vitellius on whom he could place any reliance; but even these had been reduced to a mere handful by slaughter and desertion, while the few who remained, though unimpeachable in their fidelity, were wanting in every quality that constitutes military efficiency, except the physical strength, and desperate courage, they brought with them from the north.

They were, however, the Emperor's last hope. They occupied the palace gardens to-night, feeding their bivouac-fires with branches from its stately cedars, or uprooting its exotic shrubs to hurl them crackling in the blaze. The Roman citizens looking on their gigantic forms moving to and fro in the glare, shuddered, and whispered, and pointed them out to each other as being half men half demons, while a passing soldier would raise his eagle crest more proudly, relating how those were the foes over whom the legions had triümphed, and would turn forthwith into a wine-shop to celebrate his prowess at the expense of some admiring citizen in the crowd.

One of these German mercenaries may be taken as a sample of the rest. He was standing sentry over a narrow wicket that afforded entrance to the palace gardens, and was the first obstacle encountered by Esca, after the latter had hastened from the Esquiline to give intelligence of the design against Cæsar's life.

Leaning on his spear, with his tall frame and large muscles thrown into strong relief by the light of the bivouac-fire behind him, he brought to the Briton's mind many a stirring memory of his own warlike boyhood, when by the side of just such champions, armed in such a manner, he had struggled, though in vain, against the discipline and the strategy of the invader.

Scarcely older than himself, the sentry possessed the comely features and the bright colouring of youth, with a depth of chest and squareness of shoulder that denoted all the power of mature manhood. He seemed indeed a formidable antagonist for any single foe, and able to keep at bay half a score of the finest men who stood in the front rank of the legions. He was clad in a long white garment of linen, reaching below the knee, and fastened at the neck by a single clasp of gold; his shield and helmet too, although this was no state occasion, but one on which he would probably be massacred before morning, were of the same metal, his spear-head and sword of the finest-tempered steel. The latter, especially, was a formidable weapon. Considerably longer than the Roman's, which was only used for the thrust at close quarters, it could deal sweeping blows that would cleave a headpiece or lop a limb, and managed lightly as a riding-wand by the German's powerful arm, would hew fearful gaps in the ranks of an enemy, if their line wavered, or their order was in any degree destroyed.

Notwithstanding the warlike nature of his arms and bearing, the sentry's face was fair and smooth as a woman's; the flaxen down was scarcely springing on his chin, and the golden locks escaped beneath his helmet and clustered in curls upon his neck. His light blue eye, too, had a mild, and rather vacant expression as it roved carelessly around; but the Romans had long ago learned that those light blue eyes could kindle into sparks of fire when steel was crossed, could glare with invincible hatred and defiance even when fixed in death.

Esca's heart warmed to the barbarian guardsman with a feeling of sympathy and kindred. The latter sentiment may have suggested the plan by which he obtained entrance to the palace, for the difficulty of so doing had presented itself to him in brighter colours every moment as he approached. Pausing, therefore, at a few paces from the sentry, who levelled his spear and challenged when he heard footsteps, the Briton unbuckled his sword and cast it down between them, to indicate that he claimed protection and had no intention of offence.

The other muttered some unintelligible words in his own language. It was obvious that he knew no Latin and that their conversation must be carried on by signs. This, however, rather smoothed than enhanced the difficulty; and it was a relief to Esca that the first impulse of the German had not been to alarm his comrades, and resort to violence.

The latter seemed to entertain no apprehension from any single individual whether friend or foe, and looked, moreover, with favourable eyes on Esca's appearance, which bore a certain family likeness to that of his own countrymen. He suffered him therefore to approach his post, questioning him by signs, to which the Briton replied in the same manner, perfectly ignorant of their meaning, but with a fervent hope that the result of these mysterious gestures might be his admission within the wall.

Under such circumstances the two were not

likely to arrive at a clear understanding. After a while the German looked completely puzzled, and passed the word in his own language to a comrade within hearing, apparently for assistance. Esca heard the same sound repeated in more than ne voice, till it died away under the trees; there was obviously a strong chain of sentries round Cæsar's palace.

In the meantime the German would not permit Esca to approach within spear's-length of his post, though he kept him back good-humouredly with the butt-end of that weapon, nor would he suffer him to pick his sword up and gird it round his waist again—making nevertheless, all the while, signs of cordiality and friendship; but though Esca responded to these with equal warmth, he was no nearer the inside than at first.

Presently the heavy tramp of armed men smote his ear, and a centurion, accompanied by half a dozen soldiers, approached the wicket. These bore a strong resemblance, both in form and features, to the sentry who had summoned them; but their officer spoke Latin, and Esca, who had gained a little time to mature his plan, answered the German centurion's questions without hesitation.

"I belong to your own division," said he, "though I come from farther north than your troop, and speak a different dialect. We were disbanded but yesterday, by a written order from Cæsar. It has turned out to be a forgery. We have been scattered through half the wine-shops in Rome, and a herald came round and found me drinking, and bade me return to my duty without delay. He said we were to muster somewhere hereabouts, that we should find a post at the palace, and could join it till our own officers came back. I am but a barbarian, I know little of Rome, but this is the palace, is it not? and you are a centurion of the German guard?"

He drew himself up as he spoke, with military respect, and the officer had no hesitation in believing his tale, the more so that certain of Cæsar's troops had lately been disbanded at a time when their services seemed to be most in requisition. Taking charge of Esca's weapon, he spoke a few words in his own language to the sentry, and then addressed the Briton.

"You may come to the main-guard," said he. "I should not mind a few more of the same maniple. We are likely to want all we can get, to-night."

As he conducted him through the gardens, he asked several questions concerning the strength of the opposing party, the state of the town, and the general feeling of the citizens towards Vitellius, all which Esca parried to the best of his abilities, hazarding a guess where he could, and accounting for his ignorance where he could not, on the plea that he had spent his whole time since his dismissal in the wine-shops, an excuse which the centurion's knowledge of the tastes and habits of his division, caused him to accept without suspicion of its truth.

Arrived at the watch-fire, Esca's military experience, slight as it had been, was enough to apprise him of the imminent dangers that threatened the palace in the event of an attack. The huge Germans lounged and lay about in the glare of the burning logs, as though feast, and song, and revelry were the objects for which they were mustered. Wine was flowing freely in large flagons, commensurate to the noble thirst of these Scandinavian warriors; and even the sentries leaving their posts at intervals, as caprice or indolence prompted, strode up to the watch-fire, laughed a loud laugh, drained a full beaker, and walked quietly back again, none the worse, to their beat. All hailed a new comrade with the utmost glee, as a further incentive to drink; and although Esca was pleased to find that none but their centurion was familiar with Latin, and that he was consequently free from much inconvenient cross-examination, it was obvious that there was no intention of letting him depart without pledging them in deep draughts of the rough and potent Sabine wine.

With youth, health, and a fixed resolve to keep his wits about him, the Briton managed to perform this part of a soldier's duty to the satisfaction of his entertainers. The moments seemed very long, but whilst the Germans were singing, drinking, and making their remarks upon him in their own language, he had time to think of his plans. To have declared at once that he knew of a plot against Cæsar, and to call upon the centurion to obtain his admittance to the person of the Emperor, would, he was well aware, only defeat his own object, by throwing suspicion on himself as a probable assassin, and confederate of the conspirators. To put the officer on the alert, would cause him, perhaps, to double his sentries, and to stop the allowance of wine in course of consumption; but Esca saw plainly that no resistance from within the palace could be made to the large force his late master would bring to bear upon it. The only chance for the Emperor, was to escape. If he could himself reach his presence, and warn him personally, he thought he could prevail upon him to fly. This was the difficulty. A monarch in his palace is not visible to every one who may wish to see him, even when his own safety is concerned; but Esca had already gained the interior of the gardens, and that success encouraged him to proceed.

The Germans, though believing themselves more vigilant than usual (to such a low state the boasted discipline of Cæsar's body-guard had fallen), were confused and careless under the influence of wine, and their attention to the new comer was soon distracted by a fresh chorus and a fresh flagon. Esca, under pretence that he required repose, managed to withdraw himself from the glare of the fire-light, and borrowing a cloak from a ruddy comrade with a stentorian voice, lay down in the shadow of an arbutus, and affected profound repose. By degrees, coiling himself along the sward, like a snake, he slipped out of sight, leaving his cloak so arranged as to resemble a sleeping form, and sped off in the direction of the palace, to which he was guided by numerous distant lights.

Some alarm had evidently preceded him even here. Crowds of slaves, both male and female, chiefly Greeks and Asiatics, were pouring from its egresses and hurrying through the gardens in obvious dismay. The Briton could not but remark that none were empty-handed, and the value of their burdens denoted that those who now fled had no intention ever to return. They took little notice of him when they passed, save that a few of the more timid, glancing at his stalwart figure, turned aside and ran the swifter; while others, perceiving that he was unarmed, for he had left his sword with the Germans, shot at him some contemptuous gesture or ribald jest, which they thought the barbarian would not understand in time to resent.

Thus he reached the spacious front of the palace, and here, indeed, the trumpets were sounding, and the German guard forming, evidently for resistance to an attack. There was no mistaking the expression of the men's faces, nor the clang of their heavy weapons. Though they filled the main court, however, a stream of fugitives still poured from the side-doors, and through one of these, the Briton determined he would find no difficulty in effecting an entrance. Glancing at the fine men getting under arms with such business-like rapidity, he thought how even that handful might make such a defence as would give Cæsar time to escape, either at the back of the palace, or, if that were invested, disguised as one of the slaves who were still hurrying off in motley crowds; and, notwithstanding his new-born feelings, he could not help, from old association, wishing that he might strike a blow by the side of these stalwart guardsmen, even for such a cause as theirs.

Observing a door opening on a terrace which had been left completely undefended, Esca entered the palace unopposed, and roamed through hall after hall without meeting a living creature. Much of value had already been cleared away, but enough remained to have excited the cupidity of the richest subject in Rome. Shawls, arms, jewels, vases, statues, caskets, and drinking-cups were scattered about in a waste of magnificent confusion, while in many instances, rapacious ignorance had carried off that which was comparatively the dross, and left the more precious articles behind. Esca had never even dreamed of such gorgeous luxury as he now beheld. For a few minutes his mind was no less stupefied than his eye was dazzled, and he almost forgot his object in sheer wonder and admiration; but there was no time to be lost, and he looked about in vain for some clue to guide him through this glittering wilderness to the presence of the Emperor.

The rooms seemed endless, opening one into another, and each more splendid than the last. At length he heard the sound of voices, and darting eagerly forward, found himself in the midst of half a dozen persons clad in robes of state, with garlands on their heads, reclining round the fragments of a feast, a flagon or two of wine, and a golden cornucopia of fruit and flowers.

As he entered, these started to their feet, exclaiming, "They are upon us!" and huddled together in a corner, like a flock of sheep when terrified by a dog. Observing, however, that the Briton was alone and unarmed, they seemed to take courage, and a fat figure thrusting itself forward, exclaimed in one breath, "He is not to be disturbed! Cæsar is busy. Are the Germans firm?"

His voice shook, and his whole frame quivered with fear, nevertheless Esca recognized the speaker.

It was his old antagonist, Spado, a favourite eunuch of the household, in dire terror for his life, yet showing the one redeeming quality of fidelity to the hand that fed him.

His comrades kept behind him, taking their cue from his conduct as the bellwether of the flock, yet trusting fervently his wisdom would counsel immediate flight.

"I know you," said Esca, hurriedly. "I struck you that night in anger. It is all over now. I have come to save your lives, all of you, and to rescue Cæsar."

"How?" said Spado, ignoring his previous injuries in the alarm of the hour. "You can save us? You can rescue Cæsar? Then it *is* true. The tumult is grown to a rebellion! The Germans are driven in, and the game is lost!"

The others caught up their mantles, girded themselves, and prepared for instant flight.

"The guard can hold the palace for half an hour yet," replied Esca, coolly. "But the Emperor must escape. Julius Placidus will be here forthwith, at the head of two hundred gladiators, and the Tribune means to murder his master as surely as you stand trembling there."

Ere he had done speaking, he was left alone in

the room with Spado. The Tribune's character was correctly appreciated, even by the eunuchs of the palace, and they stayed to hear no more; but Spado only looked blankly in the Briton's face, wringing his fat hands, and answered to the other's urgent appeals, "His orders were explicit. Cæsar is busy. He must not be disturbed. He said so himself. Cæsar is busy!"

CHAPTER XVIII.

THE BUSINESS OF CÆSAR.

THRUSTING Spado aside without ceremony, and disregarding the eunuch's expostulations in obedience to the orders he had received, Esca burst through a narrow door, tore down a velvet curtain, and found himself in the private apartment of the Emperor. Cæsar's business was at that moment scarcely of an urgency to weigh against the consideration of Cæsar's life. Vitellius was reclining on a couch, his dress disordered and ungirt, a garland of roses at his feet, his heavy face, of which the swollen features had lost all their early comeliness, expressing nothing but sullen, torpid calm, his eye fixed on vacancy, his weak, nerveless hands crossed in front of his unwieldy person, and his whole attitude that of one who had little to occupy his attention, save his own personal indulgence and comfort.

Yet for all this, the mind was busy within that bloated form. There are moments in existence, when the past comes back to us day by day, and incident by incident, shining out in colours, vivid and life-like as the present. On the eve of an important crisis, during the crisis itself if we are not permitted to take an active part in it, but compelled to remain passive the mere sport of its contingencies, for the few minutes that succeed a complete demolition of the fabric we have been building all our lives, we become possessed of this faculty, and seem, in a strange, dream-like sense, to live our time over again.

For the last few days, even Vitellius had awoke to the conviction that his diadem was in danger, for the last few hours he had seen cause to tremble for his life; nevertheless, none of the usual habits of the palace had been altered; and even when Primus, the successful general of his dangerous rival, Vespasian, occupied the suburbs, his reverses did but elicit from the Emperor a call for more wine, and a heartless jest.

To-day he must have seen clearly that all was lost, yet the supper to which he sat down with half a dozen favourite eunuchs, was no less elaborate than usual, the wine flowed as freely, the Emperor ate as enormously, and when he could eat no more, retired to pass his customary half-hour in perfect silence and repose, nor suffered the important process of digestion to be disturbed by the fact that his very gates must ere midnight be in possession of the enemy.

Nevertheless, as if in warning of what was to come, the pageant of his life seemed to move past his half-closed eyes; and who shall say how vain and empty such a pageant may have appeared even to the besotted glutton, who, though he had the address to catch the diadem of the Cæsars, when it was thrown to him by chance, knew but too well he had no power to retain it on his head, when wrested by the grasp of force? Though feeble and worn out, he was not old, far short of threescore years, yet what a life of change, and turmoil, and vicissitudes his had been!

Proconsul of Africa, favourite of four emperors, it must have been a certain versatility of talent, that enabled him to rule such an important province with tolerable credit, and yet retain the good graces of successive tyrants, resembling each other in nothing save incessant caprice. An informer with Tiberias; a pander to the crimes, and a proselyte to the divinity of mad Caligula; a screen for Messalina's vices, and an easy adviser to her easy and timid lord; lastly, everything in turn with Nero—chariot-driver, singer, parasite, buffoon, and in all these various parts preserving the one unfailing characteristic of a consummate and systematic debauchee.

It seemed but yesterday that he had thrown the dice with Claudius, staking land and villas as freely as jewels and gold, losing heavily to his imperial master; and though he had to borrow the money at high usury, quick-witted enough to perceive the noble reversion he had thus a chance of purchasing.

It seemed but yesterday that he flew round the dusty circus, grazing the goal with practised skill, and, by a happy dexterity, suffering Caligula to win the race so narrowly, as to enhance the pleasure of imperial triumph.

It seemed but yesterday that he sang with Nero, and flattered the monster by comparing him with the sirens, whose voices charmed mariners to their destruction.

And now was it all over? Must he indeed give up the imperial purple and the throne of blazing gold?—the luxurious banquets and the luscious wines? He shuddered and sickened while he thought of a crust of brown bread and a pitcher of water. Nay, worse than this, was he sure his life was safe? He had seen death often—what Roman had not? But at his best, in the field, clad in corslet and headpiece, and covered with a buckler, he had thought him an ugly and unwelcome visitor.

Even at Bedriacum, when he told his generals as he rode over the slain, putrefying on the ground, that "a dead enemy smelt sweet, and the sweeter for being a citizen," he remembered now that his gorge had risen while he spoke. He remembered, too, the German body-guard that had accompanied him, and the faithful courage with which his German levies fought. There were a few of them in the palace yet. It gave him confidence to recollect this. For a moment the soldier spirit kindled up within, and he felt as though he could put himself at the head of those blue-eyed giants, lead them into the very centre of the enemy, and die there like a man. He rose to his feet, and snatched at one of the weapons hanging for ornament against the wall, but the weak limbs failed, the pampered body asserted itself, and he sank back helpless on the couch.

It was at this moment that Esca burst so unceremoniously into the Emperor's presence.

Vitellius did not rise again, less alarmed, perhaps, than astonished. The Briton threw himself upon his knees, and touched the broad crimson binding of the imperial gown.

"There is not a moment to lose!" said he. "They are forcing the gates. The guard has been driven back. It is too late for resistance; but Cæsar may yet escape if he will trust himself to me."

Vitellius looked about him, bewildered. At that moment a shout was heard from the palace gardens, accompanied by a rush of many feet, and the ominous clash of steel. Esca knew that the assailants were gladiators. If they came in with their blood up, they would give no quarter.

"Cæsar must disguise himself," he insisted, earnestly. "The slaves have been leaving the palace in hundreds. If the Emperor would put on a coarse garment and come with me, I can show him the way to safety, and Placidus hastening to this apartment, will find it empty."

With all his sensual vices, there was yet something left of the old Roman spirit in Vitellius, which sparkled out in an emergency. After the first surprise of Esca's sudden entrance, he became cooler every moment. At the mention of the Tribune's name he seemed to reflect.

"Who are you?" said he, after a pause, "and how came you here?"

Short as had been his reign he had acquired the tone of royalty, and could even assume a certain dignity notwithstanding the urgency of his present distress.

In a few words Esca explained to him his danger, and his enemies.

"Placidus," repeated the Emperor, thoughtfully, and as if more concerned than surprised, "then there is no chance of the design failing; no hope of mercy when it has succeeded. Good friend! I will take your advice. I will trust you, and go with you, where you will. If I am an emperor to-morrow, you will be the greatest man in Rome."

Hitherto he had been leaning indolently back on the couch. Now he seemed to rouse himself for action, and stripped the crimson-bordered gown from his shoulders, the signet-ring from his hand. "They will make a gallant defence," said he, "but if I know Julius Placidus, he will outnumber them ten to one. Nevertheless they may hold him at bay with their long swords, till we get clear of the palace. The gardens are dark and spacious; we can hide there for a time, and take an opportunity of reaching my wife's house on Mount Aventine; Galeria will not betray me, and they will never think of looking for me there."

Speaking thus coolly and deliberately, but more to himself than his companion, Cæsar, divested of all marks of splendour in his dress and ornaments, stripped to a plain linen garment, turning up his sleeves and girding himself the while, like a slave busied in some household work requiring activity and despatch, suffered the Briton to lead him into the next apartment, where, deserted by his comrades, and sorely perplexed between a vague sense of duty and a strong inclination to run away, Spado was pacing to and fro in a ludicrous state of perturbation and dismay.

Already the noise of fighting was plainly distinguished in the outer court. The gladiators, commanded by Hippias, and guided by the treacherous Tribune, had overpowered the main body of the Germans who occupied the imperial gardens, and were now engaged with the remnant of these faithful barbarians at the very doors of the palace.

The latter, though outnumbered, fought with the desperate courage of their race. The Roman soldier in his cool methodical discipline, was sometimes puzzled to account for that frantic energy, which acknowledged no superiority either of position or numbers, which seemed to gather a fresher and more stubborn courage from defeat; and even the gladiators, men whose very livelihood was slaughter, and whose weapons were never out of their hands, found themselves no match for these large savage warriors in the struggle of a hand-to-hand combat; recoiled more than once in baffled rage and astonishment from the long swords, and the blue eyes, and the tall forms that seemed to tower and dilate in the fierce revelry of battle.

The military skill of Placidus, exercised before many a Jewish rampart, and on many a Syrian plain, had worsted the main body of the Germans by taking them in flank. Favoured by the darkness of the shrubberies, he had contrived to throw a hundred practised swordsmen unexpectedly on their most defenceless point. Surprised and outnumbered, they retreated nevertheless in good order, though sadly diminished, upon their comrades at the gate. Here the remaining handful made a desperate stand, and here Placidus, wiping his bloody sword upon his tunic, whispered to Hippias, "We must put Hirpinus and the supper-party in front! If we can but carry the gate, there are a score of entrances into the palace. Remember! we give no quarter, and we recognize no one."

Whilst the chosen band who had left the Tribune's table were held in check by the guard, there was a moment's respite, during which Cæsar might possibly escape. Esca rapidly calculating the difficulties in his own mind, had resolved to hurry him through the most secluded part of the gardens into the streets, and so running the chance of recognition which in the darkness of night, and under the coarse garb of a household slave, was but a remote contingency, to convey him by a circuitous route to Galeria's house, of which he knew the situation, and where he might be concealed for a time without danger of detection. The great obstacle was to get him out of the palace without being seen. The private door by which he had himself entered, he knew must be defended, or the assailants would have taken advantage of it ere this, and he dared not risk recognition, to say nothing of the chances of war, by endeavouring to escape through the midst of the conflict at the main gate. He appealed to Spado for assistance.

"There is a terrace at the back here," stammered the eunuch; "if Cæsar can reach it, a pathway leads directly down to the summer-house in the thickest part of the gardens; thence he can go between the fish-ponds straight to the wicket that opens on the Appian Way."

"Idiot!" exclaimed the Emperor, angrily, "how am I to reach the terrace? There is no door, and the window must be a man's height at least from the ground."

"It is your only chance of life, Illustrious!" observed Esca, impatiently. "Guide us to the window, friend," he added, turning to Spado, who looked from one to the other in helpless astonishment, "and tear that shawl from the couch; we may want it for a rope to let the Emperor down."

A fresh shout from the combatants at the gate, while it completely paralyzed the eunuch, seemed to determine Vitellius. He moved resolutely forward, followed by his two companions, Spado whispering to the Briton, "You are a brave young man. We will all escape together, I—I will stand by you to the last!"

They needed but to cross a passage and traverse another room. Cæsar peered over the window-sill, into the darkness below, and drew back.

"It is a long way down," said he. "What if I were to break a limb?" Esca produced the shawl he had brought with him from the adjoining apartment, and offered to place it under his arms, and round his body.

"Shall I go first?" said Spado. "It is not five cubits from the ground."

But the Emperor thought of his brother Lucius and the cohorts at Terracina. Could he but gain the camp there he would be safe, nay more, he could make head against his rival; he would return to Rome with a victorious army; he would retrieve the diadem and the purple, and the suppers at the palace once more.

"Stay where you are!" he commanded Spado, who was looking with an eager eye at the window. "I will risk it. One draught of Falernian, and I will risk it and begone."

He turned back towards the banqueting-room, and while he did so another shout warned him that the gate was carried, and the palace in possession of the conspirators.

Esca followed the Emperor, vainly imploring him to fly. Spado taking one more look from the window ere he risked his bones, heard the ring of armour and the tramp of feet coming round the corner of the palace, on the very terrace he desired to reach. White and trembling, he tore the garland from his head and gnawed its roses with his teeth in the impotence of his despair. He knew the last chance was gone now, and they must die.

The Emperor returned to the room where he had supped, seized a flagon of Falernian, filled himself a large goblet which he half-emptied at a draught, and set it down on the board with a deep sigh of satisfaction. The court-yard had been taken at last, and the palace surrounded. Resistance was hopeless, and escape impossible. The Germans were still fighting, indeed, within the rooms, disputing inch by inch the glittering corridors, and the carved doorways and the shining polished floors, now more slippery than ever with blood. Pictures and statues seemed to look down in calm amazement at thrust and blow and death-grapple, and all the reeling confusion of mortal strife. But the noise came nearer and nearer, the Germans falling man by man, were rapidly giving ground. Esca knew the game was lost at last, and he turned to his companions in peril with a grave and clouded brow.

"There is nothing for it left," said he, "but to die like men. Yet if there be any corner in which Cæsar can hide," he added, with something of contempt in his tone, "I will gain him five minutes more of life, if this glittering toy holds together so long."

Then he snatched from the wall an Asiatic javelin, all lacquered and ornamented with gold, cast one look at the others, as if to bid them farewell, and hurried from the room.

Spado, a mass of shaking flesh, and tumbled garments and festive ornaments strangely out of keeping with his attitude, cowered down against the wall hiding his face in his hands; but Vitellius with something akin even to gratification on his countenance, returned to the half-emptied cup, and raising it to his lips, deliberately finished his Falernian.

CHAPTER XIX.

AT BAY.

IT was not in Esca's nature to be within hearing of shrewd blows and yet abstain from taking part in the fray. His recent sentiments had indeed undergone a change that would produce timely fruit; and neither the words of the preacher in the Esquiline, nor the example of Calchas, nor the sweet influence of Mariamne, had been without their effect. But it was engrained in his very character to love the stir and tumult of a fight. From a boy his blood leaped and tingled at the clash of steel. His was the courage which is scarcely exercised in the tide of personal conflict, and must be proved rather in endurance than in action—so naturally does it force itself to the front when men are dealing blow for blow.

His youth, too, had been spent in warfare, and in that most ennobling of all warfare which defends Home from the aggression of an invader. He had long ago learned to love danger for its own sake, and now he experienced besides a morbid desire to have his hand on the Tribune's throat, so he felt the point and tried the shaft of his javelin with a thrill of savage joy, while guided by the sounds of combat he hurried along the corridor to join the remnant of the faithful German Guard.

Not a score of them were left, and of these scarce one but bled from some grievous wound. Their white garments were stained with crimson, their gaudy golden armour was hacked and dinted, their strength was nearly spent, and every hope of safety gone; but their courage was still unquenched, and as man after man went down, the survivors closed in and fought on, striking desperately with their faces to the foe.

The Tribune and his chosen band, supported by a numerous body of inferior gladiators, were pressing them sore. Placidus, an expert swordsman, and in no way wanting physical courage, was conspicuous in the front. Hippias alone seemed to vie with the Tribune in reckless daring, though Hirpinus, Eumolpus, Lutorius, and the others, were all earning their wages with scrupulous fidelity, and bearing themselves according to custom, as if fighting were the one business of their lives.

When Esca reached the scene of conflict, the Tribune had just closed with a gigantic adversary. For a minute they reeled in the death-grapple, then parted as suddenly as they met, the German falling backward with a groan, the Tribune's blade as he brandished it aloft dripping with blood to the very hilt. "Euge!" shouted Hippias, who was at his side, parrying at the same moment, with consummate address, a sweeping sword-cut, dealt at him from the dead man's comrade. "That was prettily done, Tribune, and like an artist!"

Esca catching sight of his enemy's hated face, dashed in with the bound of a tiger, and taking him unawares, delivered at him so fierce and rapid a thrust as would have settled accounts between them, had Placidus possessed no other means of defence than his own skilful swordsmanship; but the fencing-master, whose eye seemed to take in all the combatants at once, cut through the curved shaft of the Briton's weapon with one turn of his short sword, and its head fell harmless on the floor. His hand was up for a deadly thrust when Esca found himself felled to the ground by some powerful fist, while a ponderous form holding him down with its whole weight, made it impossible for him to rise.

"Keep quiet, lad," whispered a friendly voice in his ear, "I was forced to strike hard to get thee down in time. Faith! the Master gives short warning with his thrusts. Here thou'rt safe, and here I'll take care thou shalt remain till the tide has rolled over us, and I can pass thee out unseen. Keep quiet! I tell thee, lest I have to strike thee senseless for thine own good."

In vain the Briton struggled to regain his feet, Hirpinus kept him down by main force. No sooner had the gladiator caught sight of his friend, than he resolved to save him from the fate which too surely threatened all who were found in the palace, and with characteristic promptitude, used the only means at his disposal for the fulfilment of his object.

A moment's reflection satisfied Esca of his old comrade's good faith. Life is sweet, and with the hope of its preservation came back the thought of Mariamne. He lay still for a few minutes, and by that time, the tide of fight had rolled on, and they were left alone.

Hirpínus rose first with a jovial laugh. "Why you went down, man," said he, "like an ox at an altar. I would have held my hand a little—in faith I would—had there been time. Well, I must help thee up, I suppose, seeing that I put thee down. Take my advice, lad, get outside as quick as thou canst. Keep the first turning to the right of the great gate, stick to the darkest part of the gardens, and run for thy life!"

So speaking, the gladiator helped Esca to his feet, and pointed down the corridor where the way was now clear. The Briton would have made one more effort to save the Emperor, but Hirpinus interposed his burly form, and finding his friend so refractory, half-led, half pushed him to the door of the palace. Here he bade him farewell, looking wistfully out into the night, as though he would fain accompany him.

"I have little taste for the job here, and that's the truth," said he, in the tone of a man who has been unfairly deprived of some expected pleasure. "The Germans made a pretty good stand for a time, but I thought there were more of them, and that the fight would have lasted twice as long. Good luck go with thee, lad, I shall perhaps never see thee again. Well, well, it can't be helped. I have been bought and paid for, and must go back to my work."

So, while Esca, hopeless of doing any more good, went his way into the gardens, Hirpinus re-entered the palace to follow his comrades, and assist in the search for the Emperor.

He was somewhat surprised to hear loud shouts of laughter echoing from the end of the corridor. Hastening on to learn the cause of such strangely-timed mirth, he came upon Rufus lying across the prostrate body of a German, and trying hard to stanch the blood that welled from a fatal gash inflicted by his dead enemy, ere he went down.

Hirpinus raised his friend's head, and knew it was all over.

"I have got it," said Rufus, in a faint voice; "my foot slipped and the clumsy barbarian lunged in over my guard. Farewell, old comrade! Bid the wife keep heart. There is a home for her at Picenum, and—the boys—keep them out of the Family. When you close with these Germans,—disengage—at half distance, and turn your wrist down with the—old—thrust, so as to——"

Weaker and weaker came the gladiator's last syllables, his head sank, his jaw dropped, and Hirpinus turning for a farewell look at the comrade with whom he had trained, and toiled, and drank, and fought, for half a score of years, dashed his hand angrily to his shaggy eyelashes, for he saw him through a mist of tears.

Another shout of laughter, louder still and nearer, roused him to action. Turning into the room whence it proceeded, he came upon a scene of combat, nearly as ludicrous as the last was pitiful.

Surrounded by a circle of gladiators, roaring out their applause and holding their sides with mirth, two most unwilling adversaries were pitted against each other. They seemed, indeed, very loth to come to close quarters, and stood face to face with excessive watchfulness and caution.

In searching for the Emperor, Placidus and his myrmidons had scoured several apartments without success. Finding the palace thus unoccupied, and now in their own hands, the men had commenced loading themselves with valuables, and prepared to decamp with their plunder, each to his home, as having fulfilled their engagement, and earned their reward. But the Tribune well knew that if Vitellius survived the night, his own head would be no longer safe on his shoulders, and that it was indispensable to find the Emperor at all hazards; so gathering a handful of gladiators round him, persuading some and threatening others, he instituted a strict search in one apartment after another, leaving no hole nor corner untried, persuaded that Cæsar must be still inside the palace, and consequently within his grasp.

He entertained, nevertheless, a lurking mistrust of treachery, roused by the late appearance of Euchenor at supper, which was rather strengthened than destroyed, by the Greek's unwillingness to engage in personal combat with the Germans. Whilst he was able to do so, the Tribune had kept a wary eye upon the pugilist, and had indeed prevented him more than once from slipping out of the conflict altogether. Now that the Germans were finally disposed of, and the palace in his power, he kept the Greek close at hand with less difficulty, jeering him, half in jest and half in earnest, on the great care he had taken of his own person in the fray.

Thus, with Euchenor at his side, followed by Hippias, and some half-dozen gladiators, the Tribune entered the room in which the Emperor had supped, and from which a door, concealed by a heavy curtain, led into a dark recess originally intended for a bath. At the foot of this curtain, half-lying, half-sitting, grovelled an obese unwieldy figure, clad in white, which moaned and shook and rocked itself to and fro, in a paroxysm of abject fear.

The Tribune leapt forward with a gleam of diabolical triumph in his eyes. The next instant his face fell, as the figure looking up, presented the scared features of the bewildered Spado.

But even in his wrath and disappointment Placidus could indulge himself with a brutal jest.

"Euchenor," said he, "thou hast hardly been well blooded to-night. Drive thy sword through this carrion, and draw it out of our way."

The Greek was only averse to cruelty, when it involved personal danger. He rushed in willingly enough, his blade up, and his eyes glaring like a tiger's; but the action roused whatever was left of manhood in the victim, and Spado sprang to his feet with the desperate courage of one who has no escape left.

Close at his hand lay a Parthian bow, one of

the many curiosities in arms that were scattered about the room, together with a sandal-wood quiver of puny painted arrows.

"Their points are poisoned," he shouted; "and a touch is death!"

Then he drew the bow to its full compass, and glared about him like some hunted beast brought to bay.

Euchenor checked in his spring stood rigid as if turned to stone. His beautiful form indeed, motionless in that life-like attitude, would have been a fit study for one of his own country's sculptors; but the surrounding gladiators, influenced only by the ludicrous points of the situation, laughed till their sides shook, at the two cowards thus confronting each other.

"To him, Euchenor!" said they with the voice and action by which a man encourages his dog at its prey. "To him, lad! Here's old Hirpinus come to back thee. He always voted thee a cur. Show him some of thy mettle now!"

Goaded by their taunts, Euchenor made a rapid feint, and crouched for another dash. Terrified and confused, the eunuch let the bow-string escape from his nerveless fingers, and the light gaudy arrow, grazing the Greek's arm, and scarcely drawing blood, fell, as it seemed, harmless to the floor between his feet.

Again there was a loud shout of derision, for Euchenor, dropping his weapon, applied this trifling scratch to his mouth; ere the laugh subsided, however, the Greek's face contracted and turned pale. With a wild yell he sprang bolt upright, raising his arms above his head, and fell forward on his breast, dead.

The gladiators leaping in, passed half a dozen swords through the eunuch's body, almost ere their comrade touched the floor. Then Lutorius and Eumolpus tearing down the curtain disappeared in the dark recess behind. There was an exclamation of surprise, a cry for mercy, a scuffling of feet, the fall of some heavy piece of furniture, and the two emerged again, dragging between them, pale and gasping, a bloated and infirm old man.

"Cæsar is fled!" said he, looking wildly round. "You seek Cæsar?" then perceiving the dark smile on the Tribune's face, and abandoning all hope of disguise, he folded his arms with a certain dignity that his coarse garments and disordered state could not wholly neutralize, and added—

"I *am* Cæsar! Strike! since there is no mercy and no escape!"

The Tribune paused an instant and pondered. Already the dawn was stealing through the palace, and the dead upturned face of Spado looked grey and ghastly in the pale cold light. Master of the situation, he did but deliberate whether he should slay Cæsar with his own hand, thus bidding high for the gratitude of his successor, or whether, by delivering him over to an infuriated soldiery, who would surely massacre him on the spot, he should make his death appear an act of popular justice, in the furtherance of which he was himself a mere dutiful instrument. A few moments' reflection on the character of Vespasian, decided him to pursue the latter course. He turned to the gladiators, and bade them secure their prisoner.

Loud shouts, and the tramp of many thousand armed feet, announced that the disaffected legions were converging on the palace, and had already filled its courtyard with masses of disciplined men, ranged under their eagles in all the imposing precision and the glittering pomp of war. The increasing daylight showed their serried files, extending far beyond the gate, over the spacious gardens of the palace, and the cold morning breeze unfurled a banner here and there, on which were already emblazoned the initials of the new emperor, "Titus Flavius Vespasian Cæsar."

As Vitellius with his hands bound, led between two gladiators, passed out of the gate which at midnight had been his own, one of these gaudy devices glittered in the rising sun before his eyes. Then his whole frame seemed to collapse, and his head sank upon his breast, for he knew that the bitterness of death had indeed come at last.

But it was no part of the Tribune's scheme that his victim's lineaments should escape observation. He put his own sword beneath the Emperor's chin, and forced him to hold his head up, while the soldiers hooted and reviled, and ridiculed their former lord.

"Let them see thy face," said the Tribune, brutally. "Even now thou art still the most notorious man in Rome."

Obese in person, lame in gait, pale, bloated, dishevelled and a captive, there was yet a certain dignity about the fallen emperor, while he drew himself up, and thus answered his enemy:—

"Thou hast eaten of my bread and drunk from my cup. I have loaded thee with riches and honours. Yesterday I was thine emperor and thy host. To-day I am thy captive and thy victim. But here, in the jaws of death, I tell thee that not to have my life and mine empire back again, would I change places with Julius Placidus the Tribune!"

They were the last words he ever spoke, for while they paraded him along the Sacred Way, the legions gathered in and struck him down, and hewed him in pieces, casting the fragments of his body into the stream of Father Tiber, stealing calm and noiseless by the walls of Rome. And though the faithful Galeria collected them for decent interment, few cared to mourn the memory of Vitellius the glutton; for the good and temperate Vespasian reigned in his stead.

CHAPTER XX.

THE FAIR HAVEN.

IN a land-locked bay sheltered by wooded hills, under a calm cloudless sky, and motionless as some sleeping sea-bird, a galley lay at anchor on the glistening surface of the Mediterranean.

Far out at sea, against a clear horizon, the breeze just stirred the waters to a purer, deeper blue, but here, behind the sharp black point, that shot boldly from the shore, long sheets of light, unshadowed by a single ripple, traversed the bay, basking warm and still in the glaring sunshine. The very gulls that usually flit so restless, to and fro, had folded their wings for an interval of repose, and the hush of the hot southern noon lay drowsily on the burnished surface of the deep.

The galley had obviously encountered her share of wind and weather. Spars were broken and tackle strained. Her large square sail rent, and patched, was under process of repair; heaped up, neglected for the present, and half unfurled upon the deck, while the double-banked seats of her rowers were unoccupied, and the long oars shipped idly in her sides. Like the sea-bird she resembled, and whose destiny she shared, it seemed as though she also had folded her wings, and gone peacefully to sleep.

Two figures were on the deck of the galley, drinking in the beauty that surrounded them, with the avidity of youth, and health, and love. They thought not of the dangers they had so narrowly escaped—of the perils by sea, and perils by land that were in store for them yet, of the sorrows they must undergo, the difficulties they must encounter, the frail thread on which their present happiness depended. It was enough for them that they were gazing on the loveliness of one of the fairest isles in the Ægean, and that they were together.

Surely there is a "Fair Haven" in the voyage of each of us, to which we reach perhaps once in a life-time, where we pause and furl the sail, and ship the oar, not that we are weary indeed, nor unseaworthy, but that we cannot resist, even the strongest and bravest of us, the longing of poor humanity for rest. Such seasons as these come to remind us of our noble destiny, and our inherent unworthiness—of our capacity for happiness, and our failure in attaining it—of the sordid casket, and the priceless jewel we are sure that it contains. At such seasons shall we not rejoice and revel in the happiness they bring? Shall we not bathe in the glorious sunshine, and snatch at the glowing fruit, and empty the golden cup, ay to the very dregs? What though there be a cloud behind the hill, a bitter morsel at the fruit's core, a drop of wormwood in the sparkling draught?—a consciousness of insecurity, a foresight of sorrow, a craving for the infinite and the eternal, which goads and guides us at once on the upward way? Would we be without it if we could? We cannot be more than human; we would not willingly be less. Is not failure the teacher of humility? Is not humility the first step to wisdom? Where is least of self-dependence, there is surely most of faith, and are not pain and sorrow the title-deeds of our inheritance hereafter?

It is a false moral, it is a morbid and unreal sentiment, beautifully as it is expressed, which teaches us that "a sorrow's crown of sorrows, is remembering happier things." All true happiness is of spiritual origin. When we have been brushed, though never so lightly by the angel's wing, we cannot afterwards entirely divest ourselves of the fragrance breathed by that celestial presence. Even in those blissful moments, something warned us they would pass away, now that they have faded here, something assures us that they will come again, hereafter. Hope is the birthright of immortality. Without winter there would be no spring. In decay is the very germ of life, and while suffering is transitory, mercy is infinite, and joy eternal.

The sailors were taking their noon-day rest below, to escape the heat. Eleazar, the Jew, sat at the stern of the vessel, deep in meditation, pondering on his country's resources, and his nation's wrongs—the dissensions that paralyzed the Lion of Judah, and the formidable qualities of the princely hunter, who was bringing him warily and gradually to bay. It would be hard enough to resist Titus with both hands free, how hopeless a task when one neutralized the efforts of the other! Eleazar's outward eye, indeed, took in the groves of olives, and the dazzling porches, the jagged rocks and the glancing water; but his spirit was gazing the while upon a very different scene. He saw his tumultuous countrymen armed with sword and spear, brave, impetuous, full of the headlong courage which made their race irresistible for attack, but lacking the cool methodical discipline, the stern habitual self-reliance so indispensable for a wearing and protracted defence; and he saw also the long even lines under the Eagles, the impregnable array of the Legions; their fortified camp, their mechanical discipline, their exact manœuvres, and the calm confident strength that was converging day by day for the downfall and destruction of his people. Then he moved restlessly, like a man impatient of actual fetters about his limbs, for he would fain be amongst them again, with his armour on, and his spear in his hand.

Calchas, too, was on board the anchored galley. He looked on the fair scene around as those look who see good in everything. And then his eye wandered from the glowing land, and the cloudless heaven, and the sparkling sea, to the stately form of Esca, and Mariamne with her gentle loving face, ere it sought his task again, the perusal of his treasured Syriac scroll, for the old man who took his share of all the labours and hardships incidental to a sea-voyage, spent in sacred study many of the hours devoted by others to rest; his lips moved in prayer, and he called down a blessing on the head of the proselyte he had gained over, and the kinsman he loved.

After the success of the Tribune's plot, and the escape of Esca from the Imperial palace, Rome was no longer a place in which the Briton might remain in safety.

Julius Placidus, although, from the prominen part taken by Domitian in public affairs, he had not attained such power as he anticipated, was yet sufficiently formidable to be a fatal enemy, and it was obvious that the only chance of life was immediately to leave the neighbourhood of so implacable an adversary. The murder, too, of Vitellius, and the accession of Vespasian, rendered Eleazar's further stay at Rome unnecessary, and even impolitic, while the services rendered to Marianne by her champion and lover, had given him a claim to the protection of the Jewish household, and the intimacy of its members. On condition of his conforming to certain feasts and observances, Eleazar therefore willingly gave Esca the shelter of of his roof, concealed him whilst he himself made preparations for a hasty departure, and suffered him to accompany the other two members that constituted his family, on their voyage home to

Jerusalem. After many storms and casualties, half of that voyage was completed, and the attachment between Esca and Mariamne which sprung up so unexpectedly at the corner of a street in Rome, had now grown to the engrossing and abiding affection which lasts for life, perhaps for eternity.

Floating in that fair haven, with the glow of love enhancing the beauty of an earthly paradise, they quaffed at the cup of happiness without remorse or misgiving, thankful for the present and trusting for the future. As shipwreck had threatened them but yesterday, as to-morrow they might again be destined to weather stormy skies, and ride through raging seas, so although they had suffered great dangers and hardships in life, greater were yet probably in store. Nevertheless, to-day all was calm and sunshine, contentment, security, and repose. They took it as it came, and standing together on the galley's deck, the beauty of those two young creatures seemed god-like, in the halo of their great joy.

"We shall never be parted here," whispered Esca, while they stooped over the bulwark, and his hand stealing to his companion's, pressed it in a gentle timid clasp.

With her large loving eyes full of tears, she leaned towards him, nearer, nearer, till her cheek touched his shoulder, and pointing upward, she answered in the low earnest tones that acknowledge neither doubt nor fear—"Esca, we shall never be parted hereafter!"

END OF VOLUME II.

CPSIA information can be obtained
at www.ICGtesting.com
Printed in the USA
LVHW100417120522
718524LV00021B/177

9 783375 003784